THE SEX MAGICIANS

ROBERT ANTON WILSON

THE SEX MAGICIANS

ROBERT ANTON WILSON

INTRODUCTION BY MICHELLE OLLEY
AFTERWORD BY GREGORY ARNOTT

HILARITAS PRESS

AT THE ORGASM RESEARCH FOUNDATION Dr. Roger Prong, who was known by some foundation employees as "a bloody Peeping Tom" and a "horny old voyeur," was in fact very scientific – or so he always insisted as he watched the girls having orgasms.

At the laboratory, Josie Welch, already nude but with a single sheet demurely spread over her full and obviously glorious body, looked unhappy as Roger entered.

"They tell me there won't be any men today," she said as soon as she saw the doctor.

"That's right, my dear," he said with professional unction. "That part of your testing is finished. Today we move on to the part that you'll find even more gratifying."

The sheet slipped a bit, revealing several inches of round, tense breast. "You want me to try dames?" she asked with some confusion of emotions; curiosity and guilt flicked in her lovely blue eyes. "I never tried that scene before. I'm not queer, you know. But if it's for science, well, maybe . . ." She obviously was hoping to be convinced.

What a fantastic piece of hot lustful woman she was, Roger thought irrelevantly.

The Sex Magicians
Copyright © 1973 Robert Anton Wilson

Print ISBN: 978-1-952746-35-2
eBook ISBN: 978-1-952746-75-8

First Edition 1973 Sheffield House
Second Edition 2024 Hilaritas Press

Cover Design by amoeba

Hilaritas Press, LLC.
P.O. Box 1153
Grand Junction, Colorado 81502
www.hilaritaspress.com

the original 1973 paperback cover

Contents

Introduction

by Michelle Olley

Vibrations come from the Space World
Is of the Cosmic Starry Dimension
Enlightenment is my Tomorrow
It has no planes of Sorrow
Hereby, our Invitation
We do invite you to be of our Space World

Sun Ra and his Arkestra, *Enlightenment*, 1958

VIBES: those astral vibrations that emanate from the Space World – and the heart of this story – are something of an overused trope for us moderns. We press them into service for music-and-party ambience checks, hot takes in politics, sensory nuance hacks in relationships, literary criticism or the latest fat-sugar-salted, hyper-palatable candy bar. Then there's the larger, cultural *Vibe Shift*, when imperceptibly, time nudges what was once the apotheosis of the zeitgeist into suddenly looking a little . . . old hat. Flares, free love, fondue sets, bondage trousers, lumberjack shirts, riot grrrls, girl power, Instagram filters, sailor flash tattoos, Blackberrys, perma-tanned impresarios spitting bile on TV talent shows, perma-tanned reality TV show presidents spitting bile on Twitter.

Many, many vibe shifts have occurred since this salacious little paperback's first edition in 1973.

The Sex Magicians manifested in the *Golden Age of Porn* – a liminal space between the invention of photography and film, and the home video recorder – all mediums embraced almost immediately by the smut peddlers of their day. Many of the first erotic daguerreotypes were created in the brothels of 19th century Paris and London, changing hands for a pretty penny. For most people in the mid 20th century, reveling in explicit sexual imagery involved going behind the green door at your local red light district's XXX cinema, perusing the top shelf *spicy* books and magazines sold in gas stations and railway newsstands, or maybe ogling the gorgeous gals, guys and gods in classical art, if you were fancy. Betamax, VHS, PAL and NTSC soon superseded (super seeded?) all that.

In 1973, if you wanted to experience kaleidoscopic, hardcore pornographic tableaux of the sort Wilson provides in the following pages you had to vibe shift past the pulp fiction paperbacks that sex shops filled their front shelves with (also used as ballast, bought by the ton, on US ships exporting goods overseas), to the *good stuff*, usually stocked towards the back, or under the counter. In 1960s and 70s swinging London Soho, sex shop genres were HETERO, HOMO and FLADGE. (I know this because I organized a lecture about it by Dr Helen Wickstead at The Museum of Sex Objects in 2022). There wasn't a shelf for HIPPY SEX MAGIC (though there was plenty of flower power-fuelled shenanigans in all three categories). This may explain why it seems to be the only surviving book released under the Sheffield House imprint. *The Sex Magicians* was originally published by GX Inc - a mostlybunall gay porn pulp paperback outfit based in the valleys of suburban LA. The book came out at the same time as Wilson's second non-fiction work *Sex and Drugs: A Journey Beyond Limits*, published (and buried without ceremony, to paraphrase Wilson's appraisal of things) by Playboy Press (now back in print via this esteemed publisher as *Sex, Drugs & Magick*).

This debut novel also comes to us from the heady days when Wilson was making his way down the freelance freefall rabbit hole, transitioning from Playboy editor salaryman into a full

 The Sex Magicians

time, capital W, Writer. As he explained to Wilson biographer PropAnon/Gabriel Kennedy in 2003: "I spent 20 years of my life working for corporations to support a large family. A large family by American standards: a wife, four kids, nine dogs, I forget how many cats, you know, and 25 chickens and a pony at one point. And I had had enough of working in a hierarchy." Wilson quit the rat/bunny race in 1972. RAW fans will know that after writing the Great Discordian American Novel with Robert Shea, it wasn't until 1975 that *Illuminatus!* saw the light of day. You do the math. *The Sex Magicians* may have been, as some have posited, an act of sex magic to bring the Discordian opus into the world, or it may have been a prosaic act of conjuring food for the table/bowls/yard. Both things can be true at once. There is a long and honorable tradition of authors writing erotic work to support their more ambitious literary efforts; William Burroughs and Anais Nin are traditionally cited here.

The hardcore nature of the anonymous cover art puts *The Sex Magicians* squarely in the back-of-the-sex shop/girlie mag small ads camp, as does the relentless procession of pornographic scenarios which the plot tip-toes discreetly between, careful not to disturb the Matter at Hand with too much deflationary exposition. For all that, Wilson manages to smuggle in many characters and ideas that will go on to stimulate and delight his readers for decades to come. And it's *funny*. Minor spoiler alert: the Hagbardish-Hefneresque character Sput brings a novel anti-establishment twist to libertine ennui by achieving the necessary erotic frisson to achieve climax only by fantasizing about authority figures, including the Attorney General and Dr Spock. The Game of Porn Baron with Unlimited Access to Blow Jobs from Aspiring Models clearly takes its toll.

Sput reminds me of the night I had dinner with Penthouse kingpin Bob Guccione back in 1997, at the height of the nostalgia-fest that was the Cool Britannia era. (Long story short, I had been recruited to help re-invent Penthouse UK for the 90s in the style of the ascendent mens' magazines of the age, like Loaded and FHM. We failed. Spectacularly.) At the time, Guccione was convinced that the mafia still had a hit out on him and rarely left his high security mansion in upstate New York. His condition for visiting London as guest of honor for our relaunch party was 24 hour security and a bullet-proof limo. The man looked Deeply Over It – like an oversized Tony Curtis carved out of teak, drinking his Coca Cola and telling war stories to our eager minor public schoolboy publishers about his run-ins with Her Majesty's Postal Service. Not quite the *dirt* they were hoping for, I'm sure.

It's a challenge to view a piece of work which was designed to goose the libidos of domesticated primates in 1973, who most likely considered themselves relatively sexually and culturally enlightened, without falling into the Internet Scolding Mode du jour. There is plenty to cringe and ick about here in the outdated language/slurs and broad assumptions about female pleasure. We may however be missing out on some of its revolutionary sedition if we don't take into consideration how much actual sexual praxis Wilson includes in *The Sex Magicians*. As he discusses in the contemporaneous *Sex, Drugs and Magick*, there are certain practices passed through time, cloaked in occult linguistic folderol that have millennia of proven cause and effect, helping men and women pass through the crucible of desire into the union of passion, melding minds and transcendental mutual climax. The ins and outs of how women can dependably orgasm was certainly missing from all the surreptitious literature that came my way as a curious youngster. (I'm thinking here of the water-logged 1970s porn mags found in the bushes at my dad's local rugby club, and the 1980s Forum Letters paperback in the bottom of my mum's bedroom chest of drawers. Neither furnished me with the instructions on HOW women achieve orgasm, beyond '*he stuck it in her and she came instantly*' type-of-scenario).

There's a hypocritical tendency in mainstream media to dismiss and shame works of art that openly set out to arouse the reader. Sexual imagery and allusion is the water we scroll in. Sex and magic have this in common: they are both routinely dismissed, viewed as unserious work when deployed openly, but their techniques are regularly pressed into the service of capital in the more covert seductive arts of advertising and propaganda. You wouldn't know it from reading the London Review of Books, but raunchy 'romantasy' fiction (especially with magic, dragons, fae folk etc.) is having a moment right now, thanks to a combination of fanfic, avid women readers and #Booktok. For a peerless analysis of this trend, plus the denigration of women's erotic fiction and pornography in general I humbly recommend you take the time to watch Contrapoints philosopher Natalie Wynn's YouTube deep dive on Twilight. It's all the feminist theory on pornography you'll ever need, which I decided to spare you in this essay (Simone de Beauvoir, Germaine Greer, Nancy Friday, Andrea Dworkin, Jackie Collins – all the greats). And Contrapoints does it with poise, élan, and pictures.

Perhaps over time we moderns have learned to tune out this desire/shame sexual double standard from our reality tunnels without scarring our psyches? Or maybe not. Maybe it Lies Beneath, percolating into a darker undercurrent, along the lines of Wilhelm Reich's contention that repressed sexual desire can be sublimated into a masochistic relationship to power? Something that best selling author and magician Alan Moore said when I interviewed him in 2009 for *Skin Two* Magazine has stuck with me: the idea that we are meta-programmed by mainstream culture to feel shame and powerlessness after becoming aroused by mainstream porn. He compared pornography to the Skinner box (a 1930s pleasure/pain device used on rodents, invented by psychologist B.F. Skinner) that delivers an electric shock of shame and regret to us horny little rats as soon as we are *done* with the object facilitating our desire. Such a rationalized fusion of desire and shame can't be good for us in the long term. This may well be the case for the ubiquitous forms of modern pornography, delivered like most things on our smartphones these days, in snack-sized chunks of empty calories. And how does that vibe with the cognitive dissonance we all live with in a world beset with moral contradictions? Should we not also feel shame because the pornography we watch is delivered to us by a phone made by an indentured worker in slave labor conditions in the far east, containing a climate-destroying lithium chip, dug out in a perilous environment by a miner (usually a woman or child) on subsistence wages in Africa? The Skinner box in our pockets delivers a FNORD because Everything Else These Days that provides our dopamine hits also comes with a shock of shame for those with eyes to see. Ethical Consumption Is – indeed – Impossible Under Late-Stage Capitalism, as the late 00s meme goes. Numbness to our environment is a logical survival mechanism so we can go on in the world that contains such horrors as deeply unnecessary poverty, war and climate collapse. Guilty little turtles, all the way down . . .

Humanity's progress towards a more egalitarian world is frustratingly slow, but the sexual revolution of the 1960s, whilst far from perfect, played its part in kicking out the jams of shame and repression. All revolutions are messy and I for one am grateful to the hippy chicks, bra burning feminists and trail blazing beatnik beat girls who dared to show us the way, exploring the world on their own terms. My head spins to imagine the risk, courage and emotional labor of those mid-20th century days of American and European civil rights activism. It's no coincidence that all oppressive regimes police people's sexuality and women's reproductive rights. The freedom to express our sexuality (with the obvious proviso that it be safe, sane and consensual) and the right to agency over reproductive choices are newly won, and still being contested. A micro-example: it wasn't until 1974 – a year after *The Sex Magicians* was released – that women in the US were able to get credit cards in their own name. Every generation owes the freedom fighters of the past a debt of gratitude that is met, not by Amex, but by paying it forward to help the next generation

to keep on pushing for a fairer society everywhere. A lot to ask
of a 1970s pornographic paperback, I know, but what is chaos
theory and the butterfly effect for if not the boosting of those
ripples and signals that serve us whenever and wherever we
can?

The Sex Magicians is on one level a raunchy bit of late 60s
American CIS white male fantasy; a story about a cosmic
orgone wave, triggered by a bachelor machine, its bride –
and a sexually frustrated virgin's ecstatic initiation into the
arts of love. On another it's a classic Wilsonian tale about
good vibrations, agency and techniques for accelerating
self-awareness about our own Belief Systems, whilst having a
groovy, sexy time. It's love. And freedom. And silliness. We are
all free to dream within the safe space of our imagination, to
magic up audacious leaps of obscenity, shaking off the chains
of reality. In Alan Moore and Melinda Gebbie's *Lost Girls* their
opulent magnum opus of *benign pornography* 15 years in the
making, they describe it thus:

> "Pornographies are the enchanted parklands where
> the most secret and vulnerable of all our many selves
> can safely play . . . They are the palaces of luxury
> that all the policies and armies of the outer world
> can never spoil, can never bring to rubble . . . They
> are our gardens, where seductive paths of words and
> imagery lead us to the wet, blinding gateway of our
> pleasure, beyond which, things may only be expressed
> in language that is beyond literature . . . beyond all
> words . . ."

Vibes, maan. Viiiiiiibes . . .

About Michelle Olley:

Michelle Olley is a writer, editor, theater and events producer based in London, UK. In 1989, at the age of 23 (!) she became a director of *Skin Two* magazine – the world's leading fetish lifestyle and culture magazine. She instigated the largest fetish night club in the world, the *Skin Two* Rubber Ball in 1992 and interviewed various luminaries in the worlds of art and culture for the magazine, including Jean Paul Gaultier, Tim Burton, Marilyn Manson and Clive Barker. Michelle left *Skin Two* in 1996 to record with her band Salon Kitty, going on to join magazines including *Penthouse UK*, gay men's lifestyle title *Attitude*, fashion quarterly *P.U.R.E*, and pioneering gay men and women's lifestyle title, *Fable*. She has written and edited eight anthologies of erotic art and photography. Her work has appeared in *The Sunday Times*, *The Independent on Sunday*, *The Guardian* and *i-D magazine*. From 2004-2015 she worked at Turner Broadcasting, including a seven year stint as Content Manager for Adult Swim Europe. In 2014 Michelle was part of the crew that first put on Robert Anton Wilson's *Cosmic Trigger the Play,* written and directed by Daisy Eris Campbell, moving into co-production for the 2017 run of the show at The Cockpit Theatre in 2017. She's also a co-founder of the 'positive future narratives' event Journey to Nutopia with writer/musician Richard Norris, hosting several RAW-inspired events. In 2022 she revisited the world of sexual politics and history when she helped The Keeper of The Museum of Sex Objects with the set up a month-long residency at The Horse Hospital arts space in Bloomsbury. These days, she is part of the team at The Cockpit, a fringe London venue that prides itself on supporting work with *Disruptive Panache*. Her pope name is Monkeybumps the Younger (ex comm).

*Sexual vibrations spread through Chicago,
causing erotic hysteria and an epidemic of orgies . . .*

The Sex Magicians

CHAPTER ONE

What is the sound of one hand clapping?

It was early spring. The sun hung low and sultry over Chicago, turning everybody's mood in a low and sultry direction.

Dr. Roger Prong – neat, clean, rich and not yet forty – drove into the grounds of the Orgasm Research Foundation on Lake Shore Drive at precisely 8:57 in the morning. He checked his wrist watch again after he parked his sleek Jaguar in the executive parking lot. It was 8:58. Excellent. A quick trot and he was at his desk before the office clock reached nine. Once again he had demonstrated the punctuality which had contributed so much to raising him to his present high position in the medical research bureaucracy of the United States.

Roger Prong, M.D., LL.D., Ph.D., at the age of only thirty-eight, headed the most heavily funded and hotly debated institution in the world: Orgasm Research, a multimillion-dollar project dedicated to filling in the psychological intangibles left out of the pioneering research of Masters and Johnson. Since these psychological intangibles were – as Dr. Prong sometimes wittily remarked – "both psychological and intangible," there was no end to his research. Meanwhile the money came rolling in.

Roger was, according to a survey by a management analyst, one of the seventeen men in the United States who was totally happy with his job.

Other researchers sometimes expressed envy of this fact. "What red-blooded man," one of them had once asked cynically, "wouldn't be happy supervising and observing other people's orgasms and pulling down a *swift sixty* grand a year for it?"

This was somewhat unfair to a dedicated scientist. Roger Prong was truly fascinated by orgasms – as Edison was by electricity – and had an inexhaustible curiosity about every possible factor involved in every possible orgasm, twitch, itch, moan, gibber, gasp, shudder, or howl connected with that dramatic biological tremor. Even more, however, he was fascinated by lines, curves, averages, graphs and every aspect of mathematics that could be clearly visualized. The world, for him, was made up of shapes, not things; of relations, not entities. He lived in a universe of forms that could be written as equations and traced on graph paper.

Above his desk was a motto suggested ironically by a skeptical friend. Dr. Prong saw nothing funny about it at all and adopted it as his own banner: SCIENCE, PURE SCIENCE, AND DAMNED BE HE WHO FIRST CRIES "HOLD, TOO MUCH!"

As he often said in his high-paid lectures to medical societies, psychiatric conventions, YMCA's and PTA's, "It's just not true that 'if you've seen one orgasm, you've seen them all.' Why, Heraclitus – a great Greek philosopher who wrote over 109 fragments – once said that you can't step into the same river twice, because it's changing every second and so are you. Well, a man can't step into the same vagina twice, either."

Dr. Prong had supervised 23,017 orgasms to date, and his curiosity was still strong.

As he settled himself at his desk, he observed that Miss Tayl, his secretary, had already poured his coffee for him. Fine: the girl was really getting broken to the harness. Neatly, he whipped out his thermometer and measured the black liquid in the cup. 98.4 degrees. Excellent: she was learning to meet his exact demands.

Dr. Prong could not abide inexactitude or sloppiness in any

human activity. "A thing worth doing," he would explain to his subordinates, "is worth doing *right*." He said this often, and malicious members of the staff said it even more often, when he was out of earshot, with a tone and an expression that were caricatures of his own.

With a smile on his lips and a glint in his eye, Roger Prong buzzed Miss Tayl. "What's first for today?" he asked cheerfully, eager to plunge directly back into the thick of things, as was typical of him on Monday mornings.

"Subject in Laboratory Three," the secretary said in a trained and neutral tone. "An M.O."

Roger was immediately entranced. The M.O. project was one of his pet investigations. The initials stood for *multiorgasmic*, and the research was devoted to finding how many orgasms a truly multiorgasmic woman could have in a single sex session. The lack of this data in scientific literature often struck Dr. Prong as a particularly telling example of the horrible influence of puritanism in preventing important discoveries. "After all," as he said to his colleagues when outlining this project, "we know the tallest mountain in the world, and the longest river, and the biggest star in the galaxy, and where the Pacific Ocean is deepest, and who wrote the longest novel in history, and even who ate the most pies in all the pie-eating contests since records were kept on that. Isn't it terrible that we don't know the *come champion* of the world?"

It was Roger's habit to talk in racy and slangy terms on occasion when addressing foundation employees. "It relieves the tension," he would explain if a visitor was upset. "Call a spade a spade," he would add emphatically, unless the visitor happened to be black.

Miss Welch was the latest candidate for possible *come champion*. She had been fetched – along with quite a few washouts and pretenders – by an ad the foundation had placed in various underground newspapers throughout the nation:

SEXPOT WANTED

No, this is not a seduction come-on. An important
scientific project requires a woman who loves sex
even more than she loves breathing. If this fits you,
write to Box 23, Chicago, General Post Office.

$500 fee, discretion guaranteed.

An equal opportunity employer.

The neurotic, the scrawny, the unattractive had answered
in droves, and weeding them out had taken a long time. Miss
Welch – Josie, to her friends – seemed to be the real article,
at least according to the preliminary tests the previous week
in which she had exhausted ten strong men, including the
original Cuban Superman who had been found and hired by the
foundation at great expense.

Today, the real test would be given.

Roger Prong's eyes sparkled at the thought. Some foundation
employees having seen the gleam were known to remark
among themselves that the good doctor was "a bloody Peeping
Tom" or "a horny old voyeur." In fact, his anticipation was, as
he always insisted, largely scientific. He was truly curious to
see what number would finally emerge as the total number of
single-session orgasms by the world's come champion.

Twirling his dapper bow tie debonairly, Roger Prong,
physician and scientist, strode down the hall to Laboratory
Three.

Josie Welch, already nude but with a single sheet demurely
spread over her full and obviously glorious body, looked
unhappy as Roger entered.

"They tell me there won't be any men today," she said as
soon as she saw the doctor.

"That's right, my dear," he said with professional unction.
"That part of your testing is finished. Today we move on to the
part that you'll find even more gratifying."

The sheet slipped a bit, revealing several inches of round, tense breast. "You want me to try dames?" she asked with some confusion of emotions; curiosity and guilt flickered in her lovely blue eyes. "I never tried that scene before. I'm not queer, you know. But if it's for science, well, maybe . . ." She obviously was hoping to be convinced.

What a fantastic piece of hot lustful woman she was, Roger thought irrelevantly. Despite his scientific attitude, he felt himself secretly longing for the moments ahead when the sheet would finally be swept aside to reveal that incredible body which had appeared in his dreams twice over the weekend. With an effort, he resumed his professional manner.

"No," he said quietly. "No – er – dames. What we have in mind harks back to some of the early Masters-Johnson research. We intend to use the artificial coital equipment – the ACE, we call it."

"A machine?" she said, disappointed. "I don't know if I can really – uh, respond – to a machine." "You *can*, my dear, you *can*," Dr. Prong said softly. "We've never had a woman in this type of experiment who didn't express that doubt at first, and we never had one who didn't respond – magnificently. Believe me, Miss Welch."

"You can call me Josie," she said demurely. The sheet slipped an inch further. In a minute, if it kept slipping, that gorgeous nipple – like a chocolate gumdrop, he thought – would be visible. God was kind, Roger thought abstractly, to give such a horny wench just the kind of voluptuous overripe body that attracted all the men she wanted.

"First of all," he said professionally, "you must choose the – ah – penile surrogate." At her blank glance, he added "The imitation cock that suits you best." Turning, he called to one of the technicians, "Joe, bring over the sticks. That's our local slang," he added to Miss Welch – Josie, he corrected himself mentally.

He also cursed, not for the first time, the professional

standards that would ruin his career if he ever touched one of the experimental subjects.

Josie was very tempting, and she knew it.

"Here they are," said Joe, a youngster built like a bull. As always, he looked a bit embarrassed to be presenting these objects to a female experimental subject. In his hands he held a tray with five realistic-looking plastic penes upon it, in varying sizes. Josie hesitated, for once seeming to feel embarrassed herself.

"We have nicknames for them," Roger said smoothly, to distract her from negative emotion. "The little one is the Casper Milquetoast. The others, in ascending order are the Errol Flynn, the Primo Camera, the Sword of Conan, and, ha ha, the King Kong."

The girl's eyes were a bit glazed. "I'll take the King Kong," she said hoarsely.

God, what a horny bitch, Roger thought. She was obviously turning on already. He made a note on his pad: "Susceptible to visual stimuli – penes."

"Set it up," he said to Joe. The young technician retreated, the back of his neck somewhat red.

"You will control the equipment yourself," he began explaining to Josie, having some trouble in meeting her out-of-focus eyes. "By moving the handle that will be next to your right hand, you can increase or decrease the speed and also the depth of thrust. Now, the object as I have explained is to measure your M.O.Q. – your *multiorgasmic quotient* – so all you have to think about is enjoying yourself just as much as your little heart desires, ha ha." What man of mere flesh and blood, he wondered privately, could satisfy the hunger in those tense eyes of hers?

Joe wheeled over the ACE machine and affixed it on the foot of the bed, guiding it at the proper angle to give her hand access to the handle. It looked like an ithyphallic robot. The

King Kong penis dangled, impressively, just above the crotch hairs slightly visible through the thin white sheet. Joe's neck was redder than ever. "All set," he said brightly, and retreated to the door.

Joe couldn't bear to watch these performances ever since the time he had come in his trousers, to the amusement of another technician.

Josie Welch reached out a tentative hand and felt the gigantic penis hovering above her midsection. "It's not cold," she said gratefully.

"We keep it at body temperature. There are microscopic heating coils inside," Roger explained.

There was a pause. He watched her hand moving along the gigantic shaft. In imagination, he vividly felt the same hand upon his shaft. I am a professional, he reminded himself sternly.

"Well," he said. "Any time you're ready."

"I get $500 toward next year's tuition," the girl said hoarsely. "And it's for science."

"That's right," he said. "For science."

"$500," she repeated.

"$500," he agreed, humoring her. They both knew she would do it for free. He had never seen such a way-out look in the eyes of any undrugged female.

"Take the sheet off me," she whispered.

"I can't do that," Roger said, straining to avoid a break in his voice, his eyes on the crotch beneath the sheets. "You know I can't touch you or the bed in any way. Professional ethics."

"Oh, yes," she said. "I forgot."

There was another pause.

"For science," he said gently.

"For science," she agreed. Slowly, she pushed the sheet down, revealing those globes that had twice tormented his sleep. She must be at least a forty-two, he thought, and who ever saw such enormous nipples before? Then, with more determination, she pushed the sheet the rest of the way in one motion and kicked it from the bed. She was nude before him.

Josie Welch had a body, as one of her lovers had once remarked, "that would make a bishop kick a hole in a stained-glass window." From the tip of her blonde head to her lovely little toes, she was only five feet and two inches, but in that space were the breasts and hips of a pagan mother-goddess, with the waist of a Petty Girl. Her belly was remarkably flat, tapering down to an authentic blonde bush, glistening with the sweat of her mounting desire. The thighs, white as cream, were full and rounded. The lower legs tapered prettily.

But his eyes darted back again to her bush, gold and glittering, as she moved the handle of the ACE machine and lowered the penis to nudge the bottom hairs.

"Er, you can use it on the clitoris first, gently, to lubricate yourself," Roger said controlling his voice.

"I'm lubricated already," she said in a strangled voice, and the first three inches of King Kong pushed into the bush, her lips expanding around it. Those lips were the clearest pink Roger had ever seen on any woman and he felt a wave of dizziness as he identified with the machine. Her eyes, he noted, were still open for a second, but completely out of focus. Then she closed them and began pulling the handle rhythmically. She was trying to take all fourteen inches immediately.

With some awe, he saw that she had actually succeeded. My God, what a vaginal expansion, he thought. He began jotting rapidly. "Nipples fully erect at twenty-three seconds. Sex-flush on breasts and neck at thirty seconds. Subject says 'God' quite clearly at thirty-six seconds . . ."

The gigantic penis called King Kong, as the scientist was writing, was creating an uproar in the nervous system of Miss Josephine Welch, the subject. As it slipped and slid in her moist pussy, she felt as if she were floating and allowed her left hand to run down her body, over the breasts, down over her belly into the bush. Rhythmically, in time with the hot fast fucking motion of the warm shaft inside her, she rubbed the bush, while the other hand slowly increased the King Kong motion. In her mind's eye she was not having sex at all, but dancing with an attractive professor at her college. As they whirled in time to the music, she imagined his wife in a corner of the dance floor glaring at her with hate, and she pressed harder against his body, feeling the real penis in this fantasy blur-world moving harder and faster inside her. Oh, my cunt, she thought, my cunt is on fire. My cunt is on fire. She was shouting it, "My cunt is on fire." The professor's wife was choking with rage.

"On fire," she heard Doctor Prong mumble as he scribbled another note. Immediately, the professor vanished from her internal movie screen, ACE vanished with him, and she visualized Dr. Prong upon the bed, ramming his own prick into her. "On fire," she shouted again, "On fire, and I'm coming."

Indeed, she was. "One," Dr. Prong said hoarsely, making a note. He watched as the giant plastic penis stopped; she was too far gone to move the handle, breathing like a horse crossing the finishing line at Hialeah. With an effort, she summoned the energy to push the handle a few more times. Then she rested, all fourteen hot realistic inches inside her.

"It was wonderful," she murmured absently. "Not at all like a machine. Not like I was afraid it would be. The man who designed this was a genius." He noticed her hand moving toward the handle again, and King Kong slowly began to withdraw from her red and moist pussy-mouth. When it was three-quarters of the way out, he estimated, or about ten inches out, she slowly eased it back in again. "It was better than a man," she said sleepily. (He had heard that before, and he always unprofessionally ached at the thought.) "No man could be so big and so hard for so long," she added, moving it again in a slow in-and-out arc. Dr. Prong forced himself to hold his breath, trying to stifle his beginning erection by starving it for oxygen. She was moving the handle quite rhythmically. "And I can keep this up as long as I want," she said dreamily.

"Yes," he said. "That's the object. To find out just how much you really, truly, want."

But she wasn't really listening. The giant penis was moving quite rapidly again, and she was off in her dreams. "Oh, fuck me," he heard her murmur quietly once. "Oh, fuck me, darling, fuck me." Then she lost all control of her hand, and the machine stopped. Only her own spasm created the friction that drove her over the edge into insane ecstasy of coming again. He watched in awe as her hungry cunt leaped up the shaft of the giant cock again and again and again. "My cunt, my cunt," he heard her mutter in delirium. "Oh, my *darling* cunt." It was the complete narcissistic experience: masturbation without a shadow of guilt or fear. Dr. Prong envied the younger generation. She actually felt no shame about being in love with her own internal organs.

But he had misjudged the girl's romantic soul.

"What do you call this again?" she asked a few moments later, as she was beginning the slow in-and-out motions in her lovely blonde bush again.

"ACE," he said. "Artificial Coital Equipment."

"Ace," she breathed. "Why, what a lovely name." And then, as the motions slowly increased, he heard her mutter occasionally, "Ace, do it to me, baby," and "Ace, fuck me, fuck my hot cunt, you devil," and "Ace, you're so big and strong, you darling, you devil, you darling devil," and so on – girl-talk, that kind of thing – until he was practically choking in his attempts to maintain scientific objectivity and stifle his rubbery and trembling cock. Watching that adorable creature, so young, so blonde, so pagan, fucking that machine and talking to it like a lover – well, he had observed many such sessions before, but never with such a beautiful girl, or one so frankly erotic.

Josie herself, that sublime heathen, was off in a new fantasy in which ACE was talking back to her in the sensuous, somewhat faggotty, somewhat sinister but undoubtedly sub- or

super-human voice of HAL, the whacked-out computer from
2001: A Space Odyssey." All the way, Josie," he was saying,
"we're going all the way this time. All the way to Jupiter."
And somewhere the monolith theme was playing, a haunting
poly-rhythm exactly in time to the slow pulsations of her
vaginal muscles as she gripped the enormous penis, relaxed,
gripped it again, and felt it driving higher and higher within the
tenderest and most sensitive part of her. Ace was not like other
men: he did exactly what she wanted in the very split second
that she wanted it. (In her delirium, she had quite forgotten
that she was manipulating the control handle.) With mounting
passion she bucked her magnificent pelvis upward, forcing
her cunt lips higher and higher on the fourteen-inch shaft,
gibbering with raw sensation, "Oh, you brutal bastard, you god,
fuck the piss and shit out of me."

Dr. Prong's face had a curious, ashy-white color. Science and
professional ethics were crumbling. He wanted to leap upon
the bed, throw the ACE machine to the floor and take her. His
erection was pulsating and his vision was red with pain and
need. "To hell with the A.M.A.," he muttered thickly, lurching
forward.

Just then the phone rang.

CHAPTER TWO

Are you drinking the water or the wave?

The midget, whose name was Markoff Chaney, was no relative of the famous Chaneys of Hollywood, but people did keep making jokes about that. It was bad enough to be, by the standards of the gigantic and stupid majority, a freak; much worse to be so named as to remind those big oversized clods of cinema's two most famous portrayers of monster-freaks. By the time the midget was fifteen, he had built up a detestation for ordinary mankind that dwarfed (he hated the word) the relative misanthropies of Paul of Tarsus, Clement of Alexandria or Swift of Dublin. Revenge, for sure, he would have. He would have revenge.

His father had been a stockholder in Blue Sky Inc., long regarded as the worst turkey on the Big Board. (It produced devices to be used in making rocket landings on low-gravity planets.) When John F. Kennedy had announced in 1960 that the U.S. would put a man on the moon by the end of that decade, profits had soared. Markoff Chaney now had a guaranteed annuity amounting to $3600 per year, $300 per month. It was enough for his purposes. Revenge, in good measure, he would have. He would have revenge.

Living in Spartan fashion, dining often on a tin of sardines and a pint of milk from a machine, traveling always by Greyhound bus, the midget crisscrossed the country constantly, raising all the hell he could in each location and vanishing inconspicuously. Born with a real gift for electronics, his original inspiration had been connected with the WALK and DON'T WALK signs in large cities. It was easy for him to rewire them so that the WALK sign lit up when the light was red and DON'T WALK when the light was green. This afforded him much amusement, but he soon discovered that people in New York, Chicago, Denver and such metropolises were quite accustomed to nothing ever working properly; they darted across the streets whenever there was a break in the traffic and ignored the idiotic double-bind in the traffic signals.

Markoff Chaney branched out. His new inspiration occurred while strolling through Norton's Emporium, a glorified five and ten cent store in San Francisco. A sign caught his eye:

NO SALES PERSON MAY LEAVE THE FLOOR
WITHOUT PERMISSION OF A SUPERIOR
– THE MGT.

What? he thought. Are the poor girls supposed to pee in their panties if they can't find the superior? Then he reflected further. Mathematics, of course. It was part of the great plot by the statistical majority to streamline everyone and everything, to reduce even biological functions to predictable lines that could be drawn on graphs. Give the corporations another hundred years, he thought bitterly, and they'll have everybody peeing at exactly 11 a.m. every morning. This was just another part of his anarchistic and lonely struggle: the midget versus the digits.

The next Saturday he was back in Norton's and had himself safely hidden in a coffee urn at closing time. When he crept out the back door in the darkness, the sign was down and in its place an improved surrealist version concocted by himself:

NO SALES PERSON MAY LEAVE THE FLOOR
OR LOOK OUT THE DOOR
WITHOUT PERMISSION OF A SUPERIOR
– THE MGT.

Markoff Chaney returned to the store several times in

the next few weeks testing out his experiment. It was as he expected: the sign remained. Nothing signed "THE MGT." would ever be challenged in modern America; the midget could always pass himself off as the management. Better yet: there was a faint tone of irritation permeating the building now. His interpolated phrase – with its pointlessness and its emphasizing of the awkward internal rhyme in the original – bothered everybody, but in a subliminal way not open to conscious reflection. Sales, he guessed correctly, were falling off.

This was far better than the WALK/DONT WALK fuck-up. Not for nothing had he once spent a semester in Professor "Sheets" Kelly's intensive seminar on modern poetry at Antioch College. Poetry was the answer to the statisticians and averagers: poetry in reverse. The awkward, the unexpected, the idiotic. He wrote in his diary the motto of his future efforts: Insanity is the only viable alternative.

His journeys continued, and his surrealist signs were left behind wherever he stopped. Men paid large fees to enter exclusive clubs where the waiters were carefully trained to be almost as snobbish as the clientele, then felt subtly insulted by signs warning them

WATCH YOUR HAT AND COAT!
WE CANNOT REPLACE STOLEN PROPERTY!
– THE MGT.

In Dallas, he found entry to the most WASPish and expensive hobby shop in the world and left behind a terse NO SMOKING, NO SPITTING – THE MGT. The clientele, who didn't like to be considered the types who might spit on somebody's floor, fumed, but none of the employees dared to remove a sign authorized by THE MGT.

A slowly rising wave of anarchy followed in Markoff Chaney's wake. Riots erupted in Watts, Philadelphia, Rochester, a flaming picnic blanket crossed the sixties;

students, infuriated by memos they could not understand, seized college offices; older folk, driven by the same sense that there was insanity at the helm of the nation, drifted into organizations like the John Birch Society or the Minutemen. By 1970, a senate committee announced that there had been over 3000 terrorist bombings in the United States in a single year. Still Markoff Chaney was not satisfied. Everybody taller than a hobbit was on his shit list, and they would all, by God, eat turd before he died.

One day in 1972, the midget was in Chicago, hiding in a coffee urn in the tenth floor editorial offices of *Pussycat* magazine. He had an improved vacation-schedule memo with him, to be run off on the office Xerox and distributed to each editor's desk. It was sure to provoke a nervous breakdown in anyone who tried to follow the bureaucratic jargon and actually fill out a vacation request in accordance with its provisions. He was happy and quite impatient for the staff to leave so he could set about his cheerful task for the night.

Two editors passed, talking.

"Who's the *Pussycat* interview for next month?" one asked.

"Roger Prong. You know, from Orgasm Research."

"Oh."

The midget had heard of Orgasm Research before and it was, of course, on his shit list. More statistics and averages, more of the modern search for the norm that he could never be. And now the bastard who headed it, Roger Prong, would be interviewed by *Pussycat* – and probably would get to ball all the gorgeous Pussiettes in the local Pussycat Club. The midget fumed. Orgasm Research moved from the middle of his shit list to the top, replacing his arch enemy Bell Telephone.

The thought of Dr. Prong remained with him all night, as he ground out his nihilist vacation memo on the office Xerox. He was still fuming when he returned to his pantry-size room at the YMCA and slipped the bolt (installed by himself) against the wandering and prehensile faggots who infested the halls.

Dr. Roger Prong, supervisor of orgasms, and now ready to dive headfirst into a barrel of Pussiettes. The midget suffered at the thought.

Savagely, he took out his deck of pornographic Tarot cards and prepared to masturbate. The one shame of his life was his continuing virginity, for which he could see no remedy. Women of his own stature turned him off entirely (there was something incestuous about even approaching them). The giant, so-called "normal" women were the Holy Grail to him – especially the foldouts in *Pussycat* – but he was afraid to approach them.

Every time he saw a Women's Lib graffito saying STAMP OUT SEXISM, he changed the last word to SIZE-ISM; but that only temporarily relieved his emotions. His only solace was his raunchy Tarot.

He laid out a Cabalistic Tree of Life and beamed at the results: Ten of Pentacles, the Fool, the Five of Wands, the Hanged Man, Death, the Seven of Swords, the Three of Pentacles, the Eight of Cups, the High Priestess, and the Wheel of Fortune. A delightful tableau for his masturbation fantasies, especially the orgy vividly presented in the Eight of Cups. He always wondered who was supposed to receive that third guy's whang.

For a while the midget's hand was busy, busy, busy, and so was his mind. Then he shifted attention to the High Priestess, who looked much as she does in a Waite deck, except that kneeling before her was a dwarf, his tongue very busy at her crotch. Markoff Chaney became the dwarf for a while, as the Priestess became Marilyn Monroe – the idol of his youth – and his hand was, again, busy, busy, busy.

Finally, the midget was quite happy.

But when he crawled into bed and tossed around waiting for sleep, his sour mood returned. Roger Prong: I must do something about that bastard, he thought.

He turned on the light and crept out of bed to hunt in his bogus-letterhead file. Here were an assortment of official-looking stationeries, some intended to deceive the recipient, others frankly aimed only at blowing the mind.

WHITE HOUSE, WASHINGTON, D. C. said one. TRANSYLVANIAN CONSUL, OFFICE OF THE CULTURAL EXCHANGE, said another. (He used that only to ask people to report any unusually large bats in their neighborhood.)

A third, especially tasteful, proclaimed nothing less than

THE PARATHEO-ANAMETAMYSTIKHOOD
OF OMNIA ESOTERICA (POOE),
HOUSE OF APOSTLES OF NULLES,
BUREAU OF THE DIVISION OF
THE DEPARTMENT OF MISCELLANEOUS PROJECTS.

A fourth represented

FRIENDS OF THE VANISHING MALERIA MOSQUITO
(COMMITTEE TO BAN D.D.T.).

A fifth, embossed with a handsome African sculpture of a three-eyed goddess, claimed to be THE CULT OF THE BLACK MOTHER, THUGGEE SOCIETY, DIVISION OF HASHISH IMPORT AND AFRO-GENEOLOGY; this was used only on prominent white racists, informing them that Afro-genealogical records indicated that their great-great-grandfather was black and they were therefore eligible for membership in the cult. A vivid submachine gun on the bottom of the page bore the suggestive slogan, "The bullet is mightier than the ballot."

Finally, the midget selected what he wanted:

CHRISTIANS AND ATHEISTS UNITED
AGAINST CREEPING AGNOSTICISM,
A Nonprophet Organization, Reverend Billy Graham,
President; Chou En-Lai, Chairman of the Board. "Ye Shall
Know the Truth and the Truth Shall Make Ye Free."

In a few moments he produced a letter calculated to short a

few circuits in Dr. Prong's computeroid cortex:

> Dear Doctor Prong:
> When you are up to your armpits in alligators it's hard
> to remember that you started out to drain the swamp.
>
> Cordially yours, Chou En-Lai

He signed with some convincing-looking Chinese characters. That should make the bastard wonder a bit, he thought with satisfaction, stuffing the mysterious letter in an envelope and addressing it. When he returned to bed, he slept like a log.

The next morning he packed and headed for the Greyhound Station, following his own Relativity Principle. ("If you move fast enough, they don't see you.") As he posted the letter to Orgasm Research, he had another inspiration. Thoughtfully, he stepped into a luncheonette to consider it over a cup of hot java. The project would require staying in Chicago for two or three weeks, but it really seemed worthwhile. Ever since he had discovered Fernando Poo it had been on his mind, waiting only for the perfect target. Who would be better than a doctor who *measured* orgasms?

Fernando Poo was an island in the Bight of Biafra, off the coast of Africa. It was occupied by two tribes known, unbelievably, as the Fang and the Bubi (pronounced *Boobie*.) The midget knew nothing more about it than that – which he had gleaned from the *National Geographic* – but the childishly obscene sound of the name appealed to him, and he had long speculated on the results of making one typical American urgently, even obsessively, aware of Fernando Poo. "The Freudian implications are tremendous," he philosophized to himself, over the coffee. "An island that sounds like a kid's bathroom humor, and a scientist who graphs sexual spasms. Norman O. Brown would love it. Hail Eris."

Eris, the ancient Greek goddess of Discord and Chaos, was his favorite deity. One of his letterheads, in fact, was for an imaginary organization called Erisian Liberation Front (ELF), with the motto "Power to the Little People!"

"Got a phone?" he asked the counterman.

"Booth back there" was the ungrammatical answer.

The phone booth in the back of the shop bore a sticker saying THIS PHONE BOOTH RESERVED FOR CLARK KENT. The midget smiled and made a note to order some similar stickers and distribute them widely. Easing himself onto the seat and lowering the phone to his level, he dialed information for the number of Orgasm Research. As he waited, he wondered absently how the Empire State Building would look adorned with a placard saying THIS SKYSCRAPER RESERVED FOR KING KONG.

"This is the White House," he said soberly when he finally reached Dr. Prong's secretary. "The President is waiting on another phone. He wishes to talk to Dr. Prong at once."

"I – I'll connect you to Laboratory Three," the flustered young lady replied. He listened to the ring.

"King K – I mean, Roger Prong," a desperate voice stammered. Probably jacking off while watching an orgasm, the midget thought savagely. Still, that "King Kong" slip was an interesting coincidence.

"This is Ezra Pound of the Fair Play for Fernando Poo Committee," the midget said, shifting his story now that he had the victim on the phone. "Your name has been given to us as one of the leaders of the American Scientific Community and, quite frankly, we are looking for all the distinguished support we can get for our next full-page ad in the *Sunday Times*. I assume you're aware of *the plight of Fernando Poo*" he said significantly, bluffing of course (but with some assurance, since every place in the world had one plight or another).

"Oh, yes, of course," Dr. Prong said evasively. "Why don't you send me your literature and I'll give it a careful reading."

"Doctor," the midget said sternly, "if you were living on Fernando Poo, wouldn't you want *Action Now?*"

"Well, undoubtedly. Now if you'll just send me your literature – "

("Oh, Ace, darling, *darling*." a female voice near the phone said distinctly.)

There was a startled pause; the midget deliberately let it drag out until the doctor spoke again.

"Er, mark the envelope to my personal attention. You can be sure that the Fernando Poo crisis has been very much on my mind. Terrible, simply terrible. But, ah, now I must be back to my business – "

("Fuck my cunt, Ace! Oh, fuck my cunt!!!")

"Doctor," the midget said sternly, "are you *balling* while you're talking to me? Is that your answer, sir, to the desperate people of Fernando Poo?"

("Now! Now!" the voice screeched, "Jesus Christ, now!!!!!")

Beautiful, the midget thought, I couldn't have called at a better time. "Doctor Prong," he said stiffly, "I don't think you are really the sort of man who will add *stature* to the Fair Play for Fernando Poo Committee." He hung up jarringly.

Beautiful. Absolutely beautiful.

He set off for the public library and stage two of his campaign, smiling all the way – except once when he encountered one of the giant women, walking her enormous Saint Bernard, and he prudently crossed the street.

CHAPTER THREE

Who will guard the guardians?

Dr. Prong was rather pensive and preoccupied at lunch that day.

"So we take a guy like that – a meat-head with no more knowledge of psychology or anthropology or sociology or medicine or history or ethics or logic than he has of nuclear physics – and we give him a gun and a club and a can of MACE and turn him loose, my God, to 'police' the rest of us. Insanity. Total insanity."

That was Dr. Frank Foxx, the youngest member of Orgasm Research's staff and, like all-too-many young doctors these days, a bit of a radical. Dr. Prong hunched over his steak and tried to evade getting drawn into the discussion.

"Foxx," said another voice – old Dr. Heyman, still cashing in on the fact that he had once worked with Kinsey and otherwise having nothing to recommend him to any employer – "sometimes you talk like a damn red commie."

"I am merely pointing out," Foxx riposted quietly, " that our local police are *armed* and *dangerous*. The same, I presume, is true in China and Russia."

"You want to disarm the police, like in England?" old Heyman asked. "Would never work here. Americans don't have the respect for Law and Order that Britons do."

"Well, then," Foxx said calmly, "arm the public. Make sure everybody has a gun and knows how to use it. Even up the odds some way or other." "Rubbish!" Heyman cried. "That would lead to sheer anarchy!"

Dr. Prong painfully concentrated on his watery mashed potatoes.

"How's Three-A?" a soft contralto asked him. It was Dr. Harriet Hopgood, obviously aware that the Boss was bored by the political discussion. Three-A was part of the code – the research subjects were never mentioned by name in any conversation – and it designated the young lady in Laboratory Three. Miss Josie Welch.

"Very impressive," Dr. Prong said. "She had reached twenty-three when I broke for lunch, and she was still going strong. I left a psych student in charge."

"Twenty-three," Dr. Foxx said. "Incredible."

"A *most* impressive woman," Dr. Hopgood added, a tone perhaps of envy creeping into her voice. Dr. Prong darted a glance at her plump face and quickly looked away again; she was transparently wistful.

Just then, Dr. Prong's secretary appeared at the table. "A telegram came for you," she said. "I thought it might be important."

When Dr. Prong tore open the envelope he was confronted with a rather curious message:

> KING KONG DIED FOR YOUR SINS.
>
> > EZRA POUND.

Ezra Pound, thought Dr. Prong, now where have I heard that name before? Then it came to him: that fellow who called at an embarrassing moment this morning, from the Fernando Poop Committee (or was it the Hernando Foof Committee?) He looked again at the idiotic message. My God, he thought, some damn crank is trying to *put me on.*

"Arm the cops with water pistols," Foxx was saying, "and establish the death penalty for any criminal who carries any

                                    The Sex Magicians

weapon except a custard pie. Turn the cops-and-robbers game into *fun.* ”

Roger Prong looked sternly at young Foxx – a nervous red-headed man still carrying the freckles of adolescence – and said tonelessly “Misplaced humor is hostile and neurotic, I’ve always thought.”

That put a damper on the conversation, and Dr. Prong soon regretted it. Without the distraction of Foxx’s baiting of old Heyman, nothing prevented Prong’s mind from circling back, again and again, to the lovely Josie, nude, drawing the King Kong fourteen-incher into her in seemingly interminable ecstasy. Like an arrow, like the King Kong itself, his mind plunged toward that golden-haired and juicily moist little honey-snatch, hot with twenty-three orgasms....

Science, he reminded himself, is eternal self-discipline.

But the old Latin joke came back to him: *Penis erectus non compus mentis*: a stiff prick knows no conscience.

O Galileo and Darwin, did you have days like this?

He finished his meal in glum silence and found himself breathing through the mouth as he walked, with uncharacteristic haste, back to Laboratory Three. With an effort, he resumed proper breathing, even though that tended to magnify the pulsing sensations he was trying to ignore in the crotch of his trousers. King Kong Died For Your Sins, he thought, grasping at any distraction – now what the hell is supposed to be funny about that? But he found himself thinking of Fay Wray’s dress ripping as she ran through the jungle with Bruce Cabot, and what the deuce would that big gorilla have done with her if they ever had a moment alone without those constant interruptions by tyrannosaurs and pterodactyls?

The psych student, with a clear red flush on his neck and glassy look in his eyes, told him, “Number thirty just finished.”

Josie lay on her back again, the beautiful blonde body seemingly totally relaxed at last, her eyes closed. But her hand was still on the control handle and Kong was still three-quarters of the way buried in her wet snatch. As Dr. Prong looked, and tried not to stare, she murmured, "Vaseline."

"Vaseline?" Roger Prong asked, fiddling with his pencil and pad. Those nipples were almost the size of almonds, he thought.

"Vaseline," she repeated, almost in a trance. "*Please!*"

The psych student fetched a jar and handed it to her, his eyes fixed nervously an inch above her head. Dr. Prong could see the slight bulge in the boy's trousers.

"Er, you can leave now," Dr. Prong said, hearing his own voice crack on "now."

Josie was rubbing the Vaseline on the shaft of King Kong.

"Aren't you hungry yet?" the doctor asked, awed.

"I guess. But science comes first," she said with a strange crooked grin. Now she was rubbing the Vaseline into her rectum, and her rounded buttocks, Dr. Prong noted nervously, were just as lovely as her front view. Her fingers went deep, deep into the crack, massaging, relaxing the sphincter muscle; the smile on her face had almost the bliss of a Chinese Buddha.

"Perhaps you'd better stay," he said to the psyche student, hurriedly. "I just remembered an appointment."

As he handed over the record pad, he watched Josie guiding King Kong into her rosy ass, breathing deeply and masturbating her clitoris with the other hand. Her behind, sticking up in the air, and her breasts, dangling because of her kneeling position, seemed the most beautiful set of curves he had ever seen, and he was intensely conscious of the growing bulge in his own trousers, which must be visible to the student also by now.

Josie suddenly began thrusting the handle rapidly, forcing the ACE equipment to ram the King Kong up her at brutal speed. "Yes," she moaned, "bugger me. You sadistic bastard. You dirty rotten prick. Bugger me, hurt me, ram it up my ass!" The hand in her snatch was busy and spasmodic.

"Good luck," he muttered inanely and fled the scene. There was only one solution when things became this tense.

"Taking an hour or so on personal business," he told his secretary briefly, grabbing his overcoat.

In ten minutes he was at his apartment a few blocks North, dialing the phone.

"Fifi's Massage Parlor," came a familiar voice. "This is Dr. Prong," he said quickly. "My back is acting up again. Could you send Miss Serpentine for an emergency home treatment?"

"She'll be there in five minutes, sir."

He hung up and looked at his bulge. Control yourself, he said silently, beginning to relax: you can wait five minutes.

He browsed in his record collection and put "Songs of the Blue Whales" on the stereo. That was always distracting. Then, rummaging in his book shelves, he picked out a new book on the films of the thirties from a university press. Heavy stuff, to keep him from being on hair-trigger when she arrived. He opened at random:

> In Fay Wray, however, we find the White Goddess appearing in her form as virgin, and the jealous father then becomes the giant ape, Kong (who is also, of course, as Wilson pointed out in the Journal of Human Relations, 1970, a symbol of capitalistic competition, as well as being the aufgehoben of the Freudian Id).

Roger Prong put down the book, squinting. Now this was really weird: King Kong was beginning to haunt him. A run of coincidences like this made no sense at all and violated the laws of statistics on which his whole scientific mind was based. It reminded him of the absurd occult speculations about "meaningful coincidences" by Freud's old enemy, Carl G. Jung, the batty Swiss psychiatrist who kept trying to bring magic into modern psychology.

There was, of course, one mathematical system in which a random sequence was suddenly interrupted by a sequence of ordered connections. That was called a Markoff Chain.

But Markoff chains only occurred in pure number series, not in real life.

Or in books by bad writers.

Dr. Prong suddenly remembered, with a shudder, the old science fiction story by L. Ron Hubbard about the poor guy who finds out he's really living in a book by a bad writer, and that the writer is determined to kill him in the last chapter.

He took the telegram from his pocket and looked at it again. KING KONG DIED FOR YOUR SINS. EZRA POUND.

Who the hell was this mysterious Pound? Judging from the phone conversation, he had a rather high voice, like Mickey Mouse or Charley McCarthy. And he represented – what was it? – the Fair Play for Geronimo Glop Committee? Where the hell was Geronimo Glop, anyway – and how was it connected with King Kong?

The doorbell rang.

Roger Prong spoke through the intercom: "Who is it?"

"Tarantella." The voice was low and sultry. "Come right in," he said, buzzing the lock. Tarantella Serpentine came through the door, a vision of dark wild beauty. A tall girl, she oddly seemed to look like Raquel Welch and early Jane Russell simultaneously, depending on which angle you caught. Her long black hair hung loose over her shoulders and halfway down her back. She wore a red-and-rust peasant blouse, in which the soft breasts, unconfined by a bra, pressed tensely against the fabric, and below a tight thigh-clutching miniskirt which magnificently revealed virtually all of her long and shapely legs, clad in black nylon. A knowing smile curved her full, sensual lips – which always reminded him of Sophia Loren – and she said, "Exciting doings at the lab again, baby?"

"Too damned true," he said frankly. "I'm on the edge."

She smiled more voluptuously. "You probably need the Special Treatment then," she said suggestively.

"That still $75?"

"For you, yes." She wet her lips.

Tarantella Serpentine, he often thought, really put her heart into her work.

"Done," he said. "God, do I need it today."

"All tense, baby? All uptight?" she asked gently as she walked him to the massage table in his bedroom. "Don't worry: Mama fix."

"People think my work is fun," he complained.

"They don't realize how careful I've got to be with the experimental subjects. One wrong move and my ass is grass. A crucifixion, that's what it would be. Even if I lived long enough to get out of prison, I'd never have a medical license again. Honest to Jesus, I'd go crazy if it wasn't for Fifi's Massage Parlor, and you."

"Poor man," she said sympathetically as he sat on the table and she began to slip off his belt. "What was her name, the one who got you so hot and bothered?"

"Josie," he said numbly, remembering.

"Well, doll, you just close your eyes now, and I'll be Josie until you feel all better." She slipped off his trousers and began unbuttoning his shirt. "I'm your Josie, and I can't bear to think that I got you uptight and left you hanging there." She took off his shirt and bent to slip his drawers down. "Josie will give you just what you need – The Special Treatment." She bent again, lifted his penis with her hand, and gave one darting flick of the tongue up the length of the shaft. He became almost fully erect at once. "Now," she said in a low whisper, "keep your eyes closed while Josie gets her equipment from her purse."

Roger stretched out on the massage table, eyes closed, and irrelevantly remembered the Final Oral for his Ph.D. This was a much better way to do a Final Oral, he thought with a grin.

Josie was back, with a tangy rubbing lotion.

(Josie? No, Tarantella.) "Now, just relax," she said, beginning to rub it on his chest. "Just relax, and dream of Josie – or anything else you want to dream of." Her skillful fingers moved up and down his torso, relaxing each muscle separately, her voice crooning occasionally, "All better. We're gonna make *all* better." One hand went under his balls abruptly and the other began to rub the bottom of his tool. "Oh, getting *so* big *so* fast," she hummed. Then a light kiss on the eye of the penis, and the hands ran slowly down his legs, relaxing them, and began to work on the cramps on his feet. Every few seconds another small kiss would descend on the eye of his tool or the tongue would run around the rim of the head, and she murmured, "Getting all comfy and dreamy, and oh all loose and happy and oh so big and purple and hard . . ."

Roger was remembering Josie ramming the ACE into her hole, but now, recreated by fantasy, the vision included himself standing at the head of the bed and her mouth open and hungry waiting to receive his purple and pulsating cock. Tarantella stopped suddenly and said, "Just a sec, now comes the next part," and the vibrator touched his forehead. "Relax all those tense face muscles, she said softly, and ran the penis-shaped electric device around his mouth, up and down the cheek like a barber, around the neck, over to the shoulder. "Getting really relaxed now," she said. "Just dream, baby, just dream. There is no reality but sensation." The vibrator ran around his chest down to his belly, and he felt both dreamy and totally alert at the same time: the girl was a whizz with that machine. "Now, make him bigger and harder than ever. Even bigger and harder than the last time, love." The vibrator moved into his bush, circled the root of his cock several times, and then slowly, very slowly, began to climb the shaft. "Bigger and bigger," she said. It was true: he opened his eyes and this was the biggest erection, and the fattest and firmest, he had ever had.

"Now," he said, "the strip."

Tarantella moved away and turned off the vibrator. "Now," she said dramatically. "Tarantella will dance for you. Then, in a few minutes, you close your eyes and I become Josie again."

"Yes," he said. "Yes."

Tarantella's dance was part Egyptian, part modern and part her own fantastic erotic imagination. She whirled, she rotated in bumps and grinds, she pranced like a deer, she posed like a statue, she came nearer and then retreated, and finally at the end of the first movement, she unbuttoned her blouse and dropped it to the floor. Her tense and lovely breasts, now bare, moved sensuously with her breathing and she stood facing him, moving only her pelvis in a slow rotation more erotic than a burlesque bump. Then she was dancing again, the breasts bouncing in a way that kept his prick tense even though she was no longer working on it. She bent slowly backwards, her miniskirt rising higher and higher until he could see pussy hairs escaping from the panties. Then she sprang forward, stood over him, trembling in some kind of voodoo possession ritual, slowly lowering those fabulous breasts until first one, then the other, hung above his prick, bouncing very gently up and down in the very eye. As she danced away again, she was working on the skirt, and when she threw it off and stood, absolutely still, in her bikini-style red panties and the sheer black nylons, he almost thought he would climax from sheer visual stimulation. Then she was moving toward him, slow as time itself, bumping and grinding, one hand on each hip, moving the panties a fraction of an inch downward every second. When she was five feet away and the top of her bush of thick black hairs was clearly visible, she stopped entirely. Her right hand moved inside the panties and, with great effort, she kept her eyes wide open, staring into his, and she moved herself slowly, very slowly, into a climax. He saw her eyes go out of focus just before her pelvis began heaving involuntarily and sweat stood out on her face and breasts. The eyes returned to focus, although she swayed weakly a moment, and she slipped down the panties, standing totally naked at last. In a moment the stockings were off too and she danced, at last, with savage and incredible passion, a nude black-and-gold flash leaping from wall to wall, working herself up to a passion almost as intense as that of her masturbation. "Now," she screamed, "Now! I'm Josie!" and she leaped across the room, flung herself across his reclining body and took his penis all the way into her mouth.

Roger closed his eyes again, visualizing Josie, as the wet, hot mouth moved up and down his shaft, the tongue darting in tantalizing circles around the head of his tool, her throat making small moans of animal pleasure. Then, slowly her head lifted, slowly his penis came out of her mouth and only the tongue remained on him, and it began moving up and down, around in circles, way down off the penis onto his balls, back again to the head, and then the mouth was on him again. She was an artiste; her hands were busy all the time, now here, now there, finally settling under his buttocks and drawing his pelvis upward in imitation copulative movements, creating a sensation that was literally like fucking her mouth.

"Now," he gasped, hardly able to talk.

She moved up, her breasts suddenly dangling above his mouth, and slowly settled herself, very carefully, on top of him, guiding his cock into her cunt with one hand.

"The vibrator," he cried suddenly. "Give me the vibrator."

She reached beside the table and found the instrument, which he immediately placed on the small of her back. "God, yes," she cried. "Move it down." He guided it down her crack as she rode him, fucking like a tigress or panther, and found her anal opening. Slowly, carefully, he inserted the vibrator, an eighth of an inch, a fourth, a half. Her cunt became hotter and he knew she was about to climax. Quickly, he rammed the vibrator all the way into her ass, and as she bounced on him, seeming to pull on his cock with her impassioned vaginal grip, he pushed himself contortedly upward, feeling as if his burning prick was piercing into her very womb with its size and hardness as he spurted again and again and again, losing consciousness totally for a few seconds.

As he returned to awareness, she was draped over him, limp and covered with the perspiration of passion. She grinned crookedly and said, "seventy-five dollars, love – and if you come up with more ideas like that last one, I might pay *you* the next time."

As they were dressing, the doorbell rang.

"I'll get it," Roger said, feeling trim and young and dynamic again.

It was a messenger with a special delivery letter for Dr. Roger Prong. Too happy to remember the weird events before Tarantella's merciful ministrations, Roger tore open the envelope, thinking that it was probably only a note from the people at *Pussycat* who wanted to interview him.

It wasn't. It was a photocopy, made that day at the public library, of a page from the *Encyclopedia Britannica*, and it told him many interesting things about Fernando Poo, including the fact that it had been named after its discoverer, the Portuguese navigator, Fernando Poo, who stumbled upon it while looking for something else in 1472. This was underlined and a neat hand had written in the margin: *Mnemonic aid: In Fourteen Hundred and Seventy-Two, Fernando Poo sailed the ocean blue.*

Chapter Four

Why is a duck?

Half a mile away, a thin needle pointing toward the sky, stood the office of Pussycat magazine, and on the tenth floor Senior Editor Josh Dill was puzzling over the latest vacation memo from personnel. "This is the worst piece of idiocy I've ever seen," he complained to his secretary. "It looks like it was written by a computer having a nervous breakdown. Listen to this gibberish: 'Half a man-day shall not be equal to half a day unless the man is actually in the office for the full day, or half of a full day, as the case may be. (This also applies to female employees.)' What the ring-tailed rambling hell does that mean?"

"Do you want me to call personnel and ask somebody to explain it?" asked the secretary, a pert little piece who could neither type nor take dictation well but held her job because she fit the *Pussycat* image.

"Hell, no!" Dill exclaimed. "Don't stir up that pit of ding-dongs. Just put me down for the first three weeks in July and if they tell me I can't have it, I'll go over their heads and talk to Sput." Stan Sputnik was the founder of the *Pussycat* empire and still acted as both Managing Editor and Publisher as well as embodying the *Pussycat* image in all his highly publicized acts and deeds.

Dill crumbled the vacation memo and threw it in the wastebasket.

"What's next?" he asked.

"Dr. Prong. About the interview."

"Oh, yes," Dill said, turning his chair to look out the window. "Call his secretary and see if he's in."

While the secretary went outside to her desk to place the call, Dill looked out over Chicago thinking of his rapid rise in the *Pussycat* empire. Originally, he had been a movie critic, but then the newspaper he worked on had suddenly collapsed after the third typesetter's strike in two years. Out of work, he had answered an ad and found himself appointed editor of a ninth-rate imitation of *Pussycat* called *Tom*. He was underpaid and overworked (the publisher, to save himself from paying writers' fees, demanded that Dill write the entire contents himself under a variety of pen names) and he spent the first hour every day sending out resumes in desperate search for a better job. Then, abruptly, he was called for an interview with Sput Sputnik himself.

At first, he was flattered that his copy had attracted the acknowledged king of the girlie magazines.

Then he found out that he was part of a gigantic coup. Sput, annoyed and dismayed by the ever-increasing number of imitations of *Pussycat*, had decided to decimate the competition in one huge raid. The staff of *Pussycat* quadrupled overnight as every editor of every competition publication was hired away at a juicy salary increase.

Pussycat suddenly had six Senior Editors, twelve Associate Editors, twenty-four Assistant Editors and thirty Junior Editors. The other publishers found themselves confronting deadlines with nobody left on their staffs. Two went bankrupt; one committed suicide; the others took a year to get back in gear again.

"Business is business," said Sput. He liked to think of himself as a tough, hard-driving businessman, as well as the twentieth century's leading philosopher, the superstud of every girl's tender dreams, the hero of the free press, the foe of bigotry and intolerance everywhere, and the world's unacknowledged Master Psychologist. If he had known there was such a thing as pie-eating champion, he would have aimed for that title also. He considered himself a Renaissance Man.

Although Josh Dill had advanced from Junior Editor to Senior Editor in only four years at Pussycat he hardly knew Sput at all. Sput never came to the offices, preferring to work in his mansion four blocks north, and Dill only saw him on the rare occasions when he was called to that imitation Taj Mahal for a conference.

Those conferences tended to be a bit much. Like certain movie actors who are always "on" even when nowhere near a sound stage, Sput was as determined to impress his editors as he was to startle and overwhelm the whole world. For years, he had insisted on playing chess during conferences, keeping an impoverished grandmaster on hand for a stiff competition; since the grandmaster knew which side his bread was buttered on, Sput always won. He had gotten this idea from a very inaccurate historical novel about Napoleon, in which the little Corsican sociopath was portrayed as playing masterful chess while discussing military strategy with his generals and the Napoleonic legal code with his judges.

More recently, Sput had read a novel about Nero. The effect was even more disconcerting than trying to talk with him while he laboriously evaded a stale Noah's Ark trap the grandmaster had set up for him to find. He was seated behind his desk receiving a blow job when Dill had been ushered into his presence the last time. It was unnerving.

"You wanted to discuss the interview subjects for the next six months?" Dill asked, taking his seat and noting that the lady kneeling before the Great Man was a recent Sex Kitten from the mag's foldout. In fact, she was the first to appear, not in an ordinary crotch shot (they are now becoming commonplace, not only in *Pussycat* but in its imitators) but in a randy low-angle crotch-shot in which her vulva lips could clearly be seen *pouting* beneath the pubic hair. Dill had been curious how that effect was obtained and asked the chief photographer, "Were you rubbing her off just before you snapped that?"

"Nah," was the laconic answer. "We tried that, but the lips still weren't visible enough. We ended up stuffing her snatch full of my hashish stash." "My God!" Dill was astonished.

"That's why she had that far-gone look in her eyes. Stoned out of her head by the time we got it all out of her again. Bet you didn't know it was possible to get high that way."

"Wonder what it would be like to ball her right after the hash came out," Dill said thoughtfully.

"Wouldn't know," the photographer sighed. "Sput put an exclusive on her soon as he saw the test shots."

Now she kneeled, nude and covered with some kind of oil that Sput had read about in the Nero book, and carefully licked his whang up and down while he, imitating supercool, went over the interview list.

"Don't want Spiro Agnew," he said. "He's too controversial."

"But, damn it, Sput, our interviews are supposed to be controversial." Dill seemed to recall saying that at each of these conferences.

"Not *that* controversial," Sput said. "Now, here, Jane Fonda and Terry Southern, they're good. But, my God, Ezra Pound, for Christ's sake – he's a fucking *poet.* "

"We interviewed Allen Ginsberg," Dill said, watching the girl's head bobbing up and down.

"Yeah, but his poems are full of dirty words. That's different."

"Pound used *fucking* in a poem once," Dill said patiently. "And the war he was against is so long ago that it's not controversial anymore."

"Nah, nah, one poet in five years is enough. (Gently, doll, gently!) I see you don't have the Attorney General on the list yet."

"It's the same as ever," Dill explained, noting that the girl's hand was sneaking down her belly into her crotch. "He just won't give us an interview. He still says we're a dirty magazine." "Damn it, we never go beyond contemporary community standards," Sput protested, hurt. "That old bastard is a *bigot*."

"Well, bigot or not, he won't give us an interview."

"Fascist reactionary bastard," Sput fumed. "Someday I'll –" Then he brightened. "Listen, doll," he said to the girl at his feet. "You're the Attorney General – now really go to it, *like a fucking vacuum cleaner!*" The girl's head began bobbing faster, and Sput slouched back a bit, smiling contentedly.

"Reactionary WASP son of a bitch," he muttered. "That's right, take it, take it all, you foe of the First Amendment!"

"Er – Roger Prong," Dill prompted.

"Very good, *very* good." Sput was whispering, as if toking a marijuana cigarette. "You Gestapo pig," he added to the girl at his feet.

"How about Jackie Kennedy Onassis?"

"Yeah, yeah, class," Sput said vaguely. He was beginning to tremble a bit. "Who else you got?" he whispered, trembling more.

"Doctor Spock."

"Spock?" Sput asked; then he repeated, shrilly, "Spock? Spock! SPOCK!???!" He was coming. Dill realized with an embarrassed twinge. "Swallow it," Sput was roaring. "Swallow it, you *wire tapper!*"

It was a distracting conference all around, Dill thought, remembering.

His secretary was at his door. "I finally located Dr. Prong," she said, "at his home. He's on the phone."

Dill picked up his phone, saying, "Ah, good afternoon, Dr. Prong. It's a great pleasure to speak to you."

"Is this on the level?" came a tense voice. "You're not involved with that Poop or Foof place, are you?"

Dill was dumbfounded. Could the head of the best-known sex research organization in America be a paranoid nut? "I *am* speaking to Dr. Roger Prong?" he asked carefully.

"Yes, yes – but how can I be sure who *I'm* speaking to?"

"Well," Dill said, "if you have your doubts, call me back. Go through information, to check the number, and then have the *Pussycat* switchboard put you on my line. That should convince you." "I'll do just that," the doctor said. "A lot of damned peculiar things are happening today. I want to be sure you're not some cohort of that Ezra Pound character." He hung up abruptly.

Ezra Pound, Dill thought bemused. The doctor thinks an aged, 87-year-old poet living in Italy is plotting against him.

An absolute nut of the first water. A real fourteen-karat mad scientist.

Obviously, this would require great care. Prong couldn't just be discarded as an interview subject for being batty; he was too big a name. The interview would go ahead, but Prong would be handled with kid gloves.

The phone buzzed, and he picked it up.

"Dr. Prong is back on the line," his secretary said.

"Put him through." He waited, then said, "Dr. Prong?"

"Well I guess it really is you," the voice said. "Please excuse me. A man in my sensitive field – cranks and schizophrenics wandering around loose . . ."

"Yes, yes, I quite understand," Dill said, rolling his eyes toward the ceiling. "Poets always have harbored nasty grudges." He had no doubt that the doctor was as goofy as a waltzing mouse.

Markoff Chaney's strategy was already working.

Chapter Five

What is Property?

That night Markoff Chaney had a dream come true.

He was renting his old room at the Y again, using it as a base for further anti-Prong activities, and had gone out for a walk on Chicago Avenue. As he approached the intersection of Michigan and Lake Shore Drive, he was thinking about a new letterhead that would say FRATERNAL ORDER OF HATE GROUPS and have Robert Welch, Eldridge Cleaver, Robert DePugh, Jerry Rubin and George Wallace listed as officers. Perhaps he might add Ti-Grace Atkinson and make her "Chairperson of the board."

"Hssst," a voice said, "You – yeah, you, *shorty.*"

The midget stiffened in anger and whirled around. "Hssst," he said, "you, – yeah, you, *asshole.* "

"Hey, no offense," the speaker said. "I got a business proposition for you." The midget looked at him sharply: he didn't look at all as shady and unsavory as a person should look who was offering a business proposition on that corner to a total stranger.

"What are you selling?" he asked.

"Not selling," the friendly giant said. "Giving away. One hundred-fifty dollars."

"And what do I have to do for it?" the midget asked warily, drawing a little closer.

"I'm a butler," the man said – and in fact he did look like butlers the midget had seen in movies. His face was much longer from the nose down than most people's; it gave him a permanent look of one who smells something but hasn't found it yet. Most Chicagoans, the midget had noticed, look like they'd just found it and it was worse than they'd imagined. "The lady I work for is very rich. *And* very eccentric." He tried to leer suggestively: the effect was like a Bishop winking. "She has a thing about m – about you people of less than average stature."

Markoff Chaney felt his heart leap. Could it be true??

"I'm not going anyplace far from lights and police cars," he said cautiously.

"It's just down the block. On Lake Shore Drive,"

"One hundred-fifty dollars?"

"That's right. She gets these moods and sends me out looking every so often."

"I'm game," the midget said, deciding. He could feel the pulse in his temple. Au revoir ma cherie, he thought, firmly convinced that was French for "good-bye to virginity."

"There's just one thing," the butler said as they walked along. "You've got to do just what I tell you. Don't be afraid: she's not a real kink – no whips and chains or anything of that scene – but, well, her tastes are a little peculiar. I promise you won't be hurt."

"Tell me," the midget said.

"It's like a little drama or charade," the butler said, lowering his voice. He explained certain things.

"What?" the midget asked. "I don't get to fuck her?"

"But it will be enjoyable nonetheless," the butler said, "and you collect one hundred-fifty smackers for it, remember."

"Oh, well," the midget said, quoting himself, "insanity is the only viable alternative."

Chapter Six

Where did the universe come from?

When Joe Smith, the technologist from the M.O. lab at Orgasm Research, got off work that evening he was in a real stew. The passions of Josie Welch were, to put it mildly, somewhat contagious. Joe couldn't see the word "organism" in a scientific paper without reading it as "orgasm." He couldn't see the name "Donald Duck" without reading it as "Donald Fuck." He couldn't even read a menu without seeing "vanilla" as "vagina." Every time he went to the john he found himself, while holding his whang, thinking how nice it would be to rub it justa little, just for a minute or so.

I'm going to have to get another job, he thought morosely.

Joe Smith was a perfectly normal man for his era and his society. He went to church about twice a year. He had a wife who was not really totally frigid. He had two nice children who only occasionally tried to murder each other with sharp-edged toys. He hated negroes and hippies and commies because they all wanted to move into his house and eject him and his family into a tent in the park. He voted Republican in good times and Democratic in bad times. He was a thoroughgoing asshole.

Joe believed that sex was not really very sinful actually if the parties involved were of opposite sexes and married or at least seriously in love and weren't too closely related and remembered to pull down the shades. Otherwise, it was not only sinful to some degree or other but also dirty and a sign of weakness. Like all men in his society in that era of history, Joe believed that any sign of weakness was worse than sin and dirtiness together and maybe even worse than high treason or poisoning the well. Joe believed in toughness and self-control and discipline. He hadn't cried since he was six years old, never laughed immoderately, and, quite naturally, his orgasms were quick and puny.

Orgasm Research was not the ideal place for such a man to earn his daily bread.

Today was particularly bad. Joe's wife had taken the kids off on a summer vacation to Lake Geneva. Joe had the hots, badly, and there was no way within his philosophy of life to do anything about it.

As Joe walked the streets of Chicago, meeting all sorts of gorgeous ladies, White, Black and Oriental, in light summer dresses and tricky miniskirts, he was like a man walking through a restaurant while starving.

Damn it, Joe thought, they're wearing those skirts shorter every year. Even as this reflection tormented him, a breath-taking blonde creature stopped abruptly and bent to pick up a coin she'd dropped. Joe was treated to a virtual panorama – or so it seemed to him: he almost heard trumpets blasting – a panorama of luscious female ass covered only in the briefest of black lace panties.

Joe suffered at the vision and rushed onward.

He decided not to go home at once. His sister-in-law, Briggitte, who was a bit too voluptuous and somewhat easygoing in her attitudes, lived downstairs and he didn't want to encounter her tonight. He was determined to retain his virtue and his fidelity to the marriage contract.

A sign caught his eye: FIFI'S MASSAGE PARLOR. Joe quickly turned his steps in a different direction. He had heard about the extra services offered at Fifi's; he had even heard legends about the most delicious of Fifi's masseuses, the fabulous Tarantella Serpentine. "Even the smell of that creature is worth the price," Fred Foxx, the radical young doctor, had said. Joe suffered again.

Joe was now in the heart of Chicago's famous Loop, and movie signs began to add to his turmoil. DEEP THROAT, one said to him, SHE SUCKS MEN DRY. Joe understood the double-meaning all too well, and his dear Matilda, mother of his children, would never consent to such a Crime Against Nature. Another sign said ADULTS ONLY – FELLINI'S TOM SAWYER. Joe fumed, thinking of what the degenerate Dago director had probably done with the classic and clean-minded American comedy; he could just imagine the new adventures Tom and Becky would find in the bottom of McDougal's Cave with Injun Joe.

A third sign proclaimed PLEASURE GIRLS OF PORT SAID – THEY LIVE FOR SEX AND ALLAH! A group of Black Muslims, he noticed, were picketing.

Joe Smith, American, cursed aloud. He thought sexy movies were un-American but pickets were even more un-American. It seemed that the whole world, or most of it certainly, was un-American nowadays.

Finally, driven to frenzy by the temptations on all sides, Joe found a restaurant that looked dark enough to be relatively free of further seductive sights. In the back recesses of his mind, the voice of Josie Welch was still droning and muttering, incoherent and torn by unbearable pleasures: "Oh, fuck me harder, ACE, you devil, you angel, fuck your Josie."

Joe slunk into a seat by the wall in a dark corner of the restaurant – which, he noted, seemed to be called The Ore House.

As his eyes adjusted to the darkness, he noticed something more disturbing.

The waitresses were all blonde – or at least bleached.

And they were all topless.

Above the waist, in fact, they wore nothing but large golden earrings and gold medallions hanging from their necks giving such names as "Nugget," "Goldie," "Stony," "Brick," etc.

Joe hurriedly turned his attention to the menu. Everything had a fancy name: "The Prospector's Pleasure" (hamburger with French fries), "The Alchemist's Delight" (cheeseburger with French fries), "The 49er" (oliveburger with French fries.)

A waitress appeared beside the table. Worse luck, she seemed to have the biggest tits in the joint. With as much effort as a sick man climbing out of bed, Joe forced his eyes upward to her face – her eyes revealed she was amused by his obvious effort – and he gasped, "The 69er – I mean, the 49er. And a bottle of Bud."

"We don't have Bud, sir. Schlitz, Hamms or Millers." They just hung there, not doing any harm. Why was it so hard to confront them? Why did he keep on fighting the impulse to suck on them, on the pointy little nipples? Why did he imagine they were saying, "Oh, fuck me, ACE, put your cock in between me and let me rub him all over . . ."? Was he going mad?

"Schlitz," he said weakly, looking at her forehead. Even when he looked into her eyes, he could still see the tits, all big and pointy and tasty-looking.

He turned his attention to the pepper shaker. It was a model of a topless waitress, with tits even bigger than her head. He turned his attention to the menu. He read "asparagus tits" three times before it came out "asparagus tips."

The waitress was back. She'd brought those tits with her. Of course, she had – did he expect her to hang them on the kitchen wall? Was he truly mad? "We're all out of Schlitz, sir."

"Millers," he gasped. They seemed to be growing, inching closer and closer to his mouth. In a place like this she couldn't be too offended if he just took one little bite, could she?

God, you've got lovely tits, he thought. For a moment he was afraid that he had said it out loud. The look in her wise, humorous eyes said that she had heard it even if he hadn't said it out loud.

She went to get the Millers.

Joe lurched to his feet and headed for the men's room. Mustn't give way to weakness, he was thinking. What would Matilda think if he were arrested for trying to rape a waitress between the tits? What would the neighbors say?

Joe could imagine the headlines: TECHNICIAN ARRESTED FOR TIT RAPE.

Coming out of the men's room, he noticed the unoccupied Shoe Shine alcove, which was obviously still open for business. Gratefully, he sank into a chair. A shoe shine would get his mind off sex for a few minutes. Maybe he would stop hearing the hysterical chant of Josie Welch keening

"Oh, fuck my pussy, ACE, fuck the piss out of me . . ."

The chair was apparently wired, for the moment he sat down a buzzer buzzed and the shoe-shine man appeared.

Only it wasn't a man.

It was a girl.

A *topless* shoe-shine girl.

The whole world is un-American, Joe thought despairingly.

This adorable creature was wearing black full-length opera hose, skyscraper heels, a red-white-and-blue skirt cut exactly parallel with the bottom hairs of her pussy, and nothing at all from here on up.

Sitting above her as she worked on his shoes, Joe discovered that staring at her tits were actually less embarrassing and awkward than trying to look someplace else. They were smallish, comparatively, but nicely rounded and very pointy. They bounced up and down as she worked. Joe watched them bounce. He surrendered finally to the pent-up horniness in his seething soul. He felt his hard-on starting, and didn't fight it. It got bigger and bigger; it was a real peach. A jim-dandy. It practically pulsated: he could almost see it right through his trousers. Those gorgeous titties bounced and wobbled, just a few inches from the throbbing penis, and he could imagine, vividly, the penis sneaking in between them, snug as a bug, warmly worming upward, arriving finally, hotter and harder than ever, in her mouth.

"One dollar, sir." The shoes were finished.

Joe lurched to his feet and staggered back to the restaurant, almost reeling, quite fit for commitment to any nut house in the state.

Somehow, he was served the cheeseburger instead of the oliveburger. He didn't notice, munching away absent-mindedly, happily enjoying all the tits in the room – big tits and little tits, rounded tits and conical tits, tits with big nipples and tits with the cutesy-tootsy little-bitty nipples, tits in front view and tits in side view, a crescendo of tits – and accepting his hard-on, now, as a fact of nature. Perhaps he would have it, throbbing and full of energy as a young puppy, until Matilda came back from Wisconsin in August.

"Another Millers," he called.

Perhaps – he thought later – he had called for another Millers more than once. Perhaps it had been several times. He was never quite sure.

Going home on the subway, he seemed to be hallucinating mildly. Was it the beers or was it Josie Welch's voice calling to him, calling endlessly, "Fuck me again, fuck me again, fuckmeagain . . ."? Whatever it was, all the women on the train seemed to have holes in their dresses at crucial points and huge tits hung out from the top, hairy little cunts peered more shyly from below. Every tit seemed to say to his throbbing hard-on, "Oh, come in between us, big fellow." Every cunt seemed to shout, even louder, "Oh, come up inside me, all hard and hot like you are now . . ."

Joe Smith fervently wished Matilda had stayed home and sent the kids to Wisconsin alone. He dreaded encountering his sister-in-law, the voluptuous and easygoing Briggitte. Ever since Matilda had left on vacation, Briggitte's humorous flirtations had seemed less like kidding and more like a real invitation. Joe couldn't bear the thought of an adultery in the family in such intimacy that it was a cast-iron cinch to be discovered eventually.

I must be strong, he told himself.

"I am stronger," he imagined his stiff penis answering smugly.

When Joe arrived home, the only light was in the kitchen.

"Hi, Briggitte," he called from the hall in a voice suggesting a tired technician at the end of a hard day, with no time for conversation.

"Come on in," she called cheerily, "I made you a steak."

"I already ate," Joe called, trying to project the voice of a master engineer thoroughly exhausted by problems so enormous that Einstein himself could barely understand their ramifications.

"Well, have some pie and coffee. I bought that peach pie you like."

Joe weakened.

You will remain calm, he said to his penis sternly.

You will remain calm – until I get into Briggitte's hot little pussy, it answered insolently.

"Are you coming?" Briggitte called.

"Just for a few minutes," he responded, conveying the tone of the fellow who designed the pyramids if the Pharaohs had also required him to build the damn things himself, brick by brick.

Briggitte turned from the stove as he entered the kitchen. She was wearing a red negligee which set off her white skin in a quite striking fashion. Joe wondered if the nipples really were visible through the spun fabric or if he was still hallucinating.

"I just got out of the tub," she said casually. "Hope you don't mind. All in the family . . ."

"All in the family," he repeated with a laugh that sounded

insane in his own ears. She looked at him speculatively.

Briggitte was a dish and knew it. Her hair, midway between blonde and red, was worn long and curly, hanging halfway down to her pert little ass in back. Her breasts were tensely high and reminded him of the old joke about a "pair of tits you could hang your hat on." Her body was slim and pleasing, especially in this flimsy negligee. She had been married once, briefly, but after the divorce had lived in California for a few years. Since returning to Illinois, she seemed to possess some mysterious knowledge or experience which caused her eyes to crinkle humorously at some of the opinions expressed in all good faith by Joe and Matilda. And she didn't seem to believe in self-control at all. Or to be afraid of weakness. Joe sometimes imagined she had indulged in *every possible weakness* out in California – sometimes, before he could catch himself, he was apt to get involved in imagining those *weaknesses* in rather vivid detail. It was both frightening and exciting, especially when the weaknesses he was imagining involved her taking some guy's cock right into her mouth and sucking it and licking it like those French girls do – and here he was imagining that again, damn it!

Briggitte leaned over from behind him to pour the coffee. One soft, round breast nuzzled his shoulder as she poured. "Have a *hard* day?" she asked. He wondered why she pronounced it that way. Sitting as he was it must be impossible for her to see that his cock was getting stiff again.

"So-so," he said noncommittally, digging into the pie.

Briggitte sat across from him and began cutting her steak. Her eyes wide with seeming innocence, she asked, "I suppose any job has its *ups* and *downs* – especially at Orgasm Research?"

"Er, yeah," he replied.

"I think it's wonderful," she gushed, "that so many girls are willing to come in there and make a *clean breast* of everything, just for the sake of scientific knowledge. Maybe I'll volunteer sometime myself."

"Mm," he offered vaguely, not sure how to field that one.

"It must make you guys feel awfully *cocky*, to know so many intimate secrets," she went on, still all innocence. The smile in her eyes knew exactly what effect this line of conversation was having.

"A scientist," Joe pronounced, "must have integrity. That goes even for a technician like me."

"Integrity is a good thing," Briggitte said carefully, "but don't get too *stiff*-necked and *stuck*-up about it."

"I'm not stiff and fucked-up," he cried frantically. "I mean – I'm not stiff-necked and sucked-up – I mean – oh, to hell with it." Her smile was maddening.

"Oh," she said softly, "you're all *prickly* and nervous tonight. I wish I could think of something to relax you."

"I'll be okay," he said briefly.

"I just hate to think," she responded, still soft and lazy and mocking, "that you're all tense and miserable just because Matilda went and left you for the summer. I mean, I can do the cooking and the laundry and like that, but if there's something else, something you especially miss –"

"No," he said. "I'm doing fine." He finished the pie and turned in his chair before rising, not wanting to face her when he stood up. "Think I'll turn in," he said vaguely.

"Poor man," she said, "all alone in that big bed."

Joe lurched to his bedroom. As he got into his pajamas, he could hear her clattering away in the kitchen. Hear her – hell, he could see her, as if the walls were glass. The red negligee flapped loosely as she washed the dishes. Every time she moved, a titty bulged suggestively at him. Joe snapped out the light and climbed between the sheets, keeping his hands above his waist, far away from his throbbing prick.

I will be strong, he thought. I will be strong. I will be strong.

The door opened.

"Joe," Briggitte said breathlessly, "I think there's somebody on the back porch. A burglar."

Joe paddled out to the kitchen and looked through the back door. Of course, there was nobody there.

"It's your nerves," he said. "I'm not the only one who's tense tonight."

He started back toward his bedroom.

"Joe," she said. "Maybe he'll come back."

"If he does, call me again." Joe lurched back to his bed.

I will be strong. I will be strong. I will be strong.

The door opened again.

"Can I borrow something to read?" Briggitte asked.

Joe was immediately aware that none of the previous temptations had prepared him for this. He was in bed. She was two feet away, looking at the bookshelves, in an increasingly transparent negligee. His hard-on seemed bigger than the John Hancock Building. Any second she might claim to feel an earthquake tremor and fall into the bed on top of him.

I will be strong. I will be strong . . .

"Oh, *Pussycat* magazine," she said. "I *love* to read that."

She flipped it open to the Pussycat of the Month.

"Damn it," she said. "She's prettier than me. Why are those girls always prettier than me?" She held the nude photo directly in front of his face. "Isn't she prettier than me?"

"No," he said, choking. "No, I don't think she's really prettier than you."

"Really? But look at those breasts. So pert and tiny they are, so cute. Not all huge and cow-like the way I am." She held the picture next to her own breasts. "See?"

"You're not cow-like" Joe objected finally, when it was obvious that he had to say something. "Big breasts are attractive, too."

"Oh, what a nice thing to say!" She dropped the magazine, leaned forward and kissed his forehead. "You're a sweet man, Joe."

"Er, we shouldn't – " he began.

"My God, what a hard-on you've got!" she interrupted.

Joe blushed beet-red. "It'll go away," he offered inanely.

"Oh, you poor, *poor* man. And you're too shy to ask me to help you with it." Her eyes were all sympathy and generosity.

"That wouldn't be right," Joe said awkwardly, wishing she'd get the hell off the bed. "What if Matilda ever found out –"

"Oh, *I* wouldn't tell her. Would you?"

"Of course not!"

'Then she won't find out."

"But," Joe protested one more time, weakly, "adultery is a serious matter –"

"Oh, foof!!!" Briggitte pronounced harshly. "That's just plain *silly*, Joe. You're very, very horny." She touched his penis lightly. "Why it's hard as a rock –" and with bright innocent eyes – "and to tell you the God's truth, I'm horny, too. And there's only one obvious remedy."

"But," Joe said, "what about will power? What about poor Matilda? What about civilization and human dignity?"

"Oh, *foof*," she said again, vexed. "You're an old fuddy-duddy! Honest, you people who never leave the Midwest are so provincial. Why, if you don't fuck me, Joe, I'll just have to rub myself off. Is that what you want to drive me to?"

"Why not?" Joe cried desperately, "at least, it's not adultery."

"You sure are a technical bastard," Briggitte said angrily. "Well, if you feel that way, that's what I'll do." And she flung herself from the bed and flounced from the room.

Joe stared at the wall. He thought of Matilda. He thought of the neighbors. He thought of God, and the reports from all the experts on God whom he had ever heard, which insisted God was extremely narrow-minded and intolerant about adultery. He thought of Briggitte downstairs in her own room, playing with her pussy, fingering it languorously and deliciously, until she made herself come. He thought of her pussy and of fingers moving around inside it. He thought of how hot his hard-on felt.

"Briggitte," he called, "wait a minute."

"Fuck you, buster!" came her inelegant reply from the staircase.

Joe got up and paddled to the hall. Downstairs, Briggitte's door slammed angrily.

Damn, blast and thunder, he thought.

He paddled downstairs in his bare feet and knocked on her door. "Briggitte?"

"Buzz off!" she shouted.

"You can't do this to me," Joe shouted back. "You have aroused the beast in me. You can't leave me this way."

"Go jack yourself off and save civilization from adultery, you *schmuck*!!!"

Joe opened the door.

Briggitte's negligee lay on the floor, crumpled, between the door and the bed.

On the bed, stark naked, Briggitte was sprawled, her legs spread wide – offering him a breathtaking view of blonde-red pussy – and with her right hand she held a peeled banana to her mouth while with her left hand she held another peeled banana to her clitoris.

"My God," he said, totally shocked.

"Don't you touch me," she warned. "Don't take a step, you self-righteous prude! You can watch me – in fact, I'd like that, especially if you jack yourself off while you're watching. But I won't let you touch me. You had your chance, buster." And with that the shameless creature took the banana back into her mouth and began sucking on it with the most voluptuous enjoyment. Joe gasped, and watched her play the other banana delicately against her clitoris, moving her pelvis in a slow bump-and-grind motion to add to the friction.

"Wait," he cried, "please –"

But she went on rubbing her pussy with the banana, gradually working it into her vagina, fucking upwards and taking it again and again all the way up inside her cunt, all the while sucking the other banana with sighs and moans of delight. Joe was wrecked, mentally. Slowly he began fingering up and down his penis, watching this lovely woman play at suck-and-fuck with her two bananas, identifying his penis with each banana alternately, imagining that he was rubbing it into her mouth one minute and then into her cunt the next minute, maddened by the moans and heaves she frankly allowed as her pleasure mounted and mounted, until he couldn't stand it and lurched forward, throwing himself upon her.

"Good," she grinned crookedly, dropping the bananas, "now you know it's really your decision." And she wriggled around, taking his penis in her mouth, offering her pussy to his tongue. Joe Smith surrendered to un-Americanism. He began licking her outer lips and worked his way gently inward toward her clitoris. In a moment, she exploded against him, fucking his mouth wildly, spasming again and again, almost biting his penis in her delirium. Then, she turned and moved around on the bed, grinning. "That will do as an overture," she said. "Now let's see if you can fuck me as good as you sucked me." Joe drove his penis into her cunt, muttering thickly, "To hell with Matilda. To hell with Mayor Daly. To hell with *everything*. I'm gonna fuck your ass off tonight!" She dug her fingers into his back, whispering, "Harder, harder . . ." He fucked as wide a swing as he could, pulling himself almost entirely out on each upper and ramming violently inward toward her womb on each downer. Her pussy was as hot and wet as cooked liver and she pressed her titties against his chest. "Give me a finger," she whispered. He shifted his weight, rested upon his elbows and held a hand to her mouth. She began sucking raptly on his middle finger, obviously pretending it was a cock, and her cunt grabbed at his real penis more ravenously, sucking it up the very heart of her as she climaxed again and again and again, and he spurted his come high, high, high within her, fucking madly and happily without a fear or worry left in his head.

Joe Smith had become the subject of a *Mama Vibe*, without even knowing what was happening to him.

CHAPTER SEVEN

Time: is it real or illusory?

After a bad start, the association between Josh Dill and Dr. Prong was going swimmingly.

"You can't do an interview in depth," Dill had explained, "until you relax and know one another. Let me take you as my guest to the Pussycat Club tonight. Bring your wife or girl friend. Hell," he added whimsically, "bring both of them if you want. "

Dr. Prong, who had neither wife nor steady girl friend, brought Tarantella Serpentine instead. In a low-cut silver evening gown that revealed most of her enormous breasts and hugged her ass tightly, she was stunning; she was a girl who wouldn't be toiling in that massage parlor for much longer, he thought. Destiny obviously meant her for bigger and better things.

Dill – to Prong's surprise – brought a girl who, despite her good looks and fashionable evening gown, revealed as soon as she opened her mouth that she was some kind of hippie or yippie. Also, she definitely seemed to be under the influence of some sort of drug: "Cool," she said, and "crazy," and "far out." Her name, Dill had said, was Stella Only.

When she spoke a whole sentence, it always ended with "and all that shit."

The evening, however, was going pleasantly. The drinks at the Pussycat Club were both strong and tasty, the Pussiette who served them had stunning long legs and a very brief costume,

the steak was good, and Dill talked very entertainingly
about his obsession, the horror films of the 1930s. ("I dig
Frankenstein and all that shit," Miss Only said occasionally, her
only other memorable remark was, on declining a third martini,
"I don't like to go too far with consciousness-contracting
drugs. It louses up the yin and yang balance and all that shit.")

"Sput is having a party tonight," Dill announced after dinner.
"Why don't we all fall up to the mansion? You'd like it, Dr.
Prong."

Swimming in the glow of his fifth Black Russian, Dr. Prong
said, "Call me Roger. I'd love to see Sput's famous mansion."

"Me too," Tarantella agreed. "I want to take everything off
and dive into that famous pool."

"Well, that's the kind of party it is," Dill said jovially. "Let's
go."

"Far fucking out," Miss Only said.

Dill signed the tab and they went out on the street and began
walking north.

"I'm going to be *inside* the Pussycat Mansion," Tarantella
said. "It's like a dream come true."

"Out of fucking sight," Miss Only agreed. Dropping back,
Dr. Prong murmured to Dill, "Is she on drugs?"

"Drugs?" Dill was startled. "Hell no. Well, maybe a little
pot."

Dr. Prong frowned his disapproval of this casual attitude
toward law breaking. "How did you ever meet her?" he asked.

"She was the Sex Kitten of the month. In May." Dr. Prong
stared at Miss Only again. It was incredible, but with her mouth
shut and those *young* words not coming out of her, she was
indeed a beautiful creature. And she wore her gown well.

"Miss Only," he said to her, "are you a professional model?"

"My name isn't Only," she said. "It's Stella. Only Stella. No
last name."

Roger Prong looked at her dubiously. The small group now contained two people who regarded two other people as being definitely bananas.

"Why should a woman have a last name?" She explained Socratically. "What last name? Her father's? Her husband's, if she has a husband? All that shit? You dig?"

"Are you a women's liberationist? Or a White Muslim? Or something?" he asked in confusion.

"I'm Stella. Only Stella," she said firmly.

A man who looked like a butler and another man who was a midget passed them.

"Teddy *Snowcrop*?" they heard the midget ask.

"I wonder what that was about," Dill said idly.

"I remember Teddy Snowcrop," Tarantella said. "A little white bear that used to be in TV commercials. Must have been a kid, or a midget, in a bear suit, I guess."

"Maybe they're going to revive it, and that guy is being hired," Dill said absently.

They turned into the courtyard of the Pussycat Mansion.

"From outside," Stella said, "it looks like any other mansion of the Drive. But wait'll you get inside, honey," she added, hugging Tarantella affectionately. "Far fucking *out.* "

The door bore a motto in Greek: ELEUTHYRIA.

"What's that mean?" Dr. Prong asked, assaying a weak jest by adding, "It's all Greek to me."

"Freedom," Dill translated, ringing the bell.

A speaker in the wall said nasally, "Identify yourself please."

"Dill," said Dill. "Three guests." He added to the others, "That's a computer. It works on voice print. Much safer than a closed-circuit TV. No two voice prints are alike, you know."

"Scientific," Stella added with awe. "Electronics and all that shit."

"Please come in," the nasal voice said, followed by a buzz.

Dill opened the door and ushered them into a foyer with a suit of armor to which Sput has impishly added a grotesquely large aluminum penis. "One of Sput's jokes," he explained wanly.

Dr. Prong suddenly remembered Josie and wondered if she was finally finished with ACE.

They went through the foyer and up a flight of stairs, passing a handsome and quite authentic Renoir original. "Sexy," Tarantella said, impressed by the realism of the flesh tones.

They entered a ballroom full of people. A large number of the women were totally nude – Pussiettes from the club, appearing for Sput's guests just as the club patrons always fantasized seeing them and acting as cocktail waitresses. They passed a Greek vase nearly five feet tall bearing a portrait of a nymph fleeing from a satyr who sported a determined grin and a convincing erection. At the right of the room – not standing and drinking, but sitting and smoking from a large hookah – were Sput and a small circle of friends, quite comfy on enormous floor pillows. Above them on the wall was an Andy Warhol original- one hundred Campbell Soup cans.

"Freedom," Sput was saying, "is the most terrifying thing in the world. Fact. People will go to any length to convince themselves they're not free. If they can't convince themselves they're being watched by the cops, they'll worry about the neighbors. Put them in the wilderness, hundreds of miles from other people, and they'll regress to childhood and start worrying that the Old Man in the Sky is watching them. Anything, no matter how irrational, to avoid doing what they want to do. Just so they can think they're acting under compulsion and, hence, aren't really responsible for what they do. Why was Hitler obeyed? Easy: anybody can be obeyed. People stand around waiting for orders if the boss is out of the room." He paused and took a thoughtful toke on the hookah.

"What's that – Turkish tobacco?" Dr. Prong asked.

"Er, yes," Dill said. "Turkish tobacco."

"Here we have freedom," Sput said. "Any vice squad or narcotics cop who bucks the political machine and tries to pull a raid will never get past the voice print on the door – not until we have time to clean up and hide the evidence, anyway. So everybody here is free. And what are they doing? Same as any other party. Waiting for me to do something outrageous first, so they can then follow suit. It's depressing."

"Sput," Dill said in the pause, "I'd like you to meet Dr. Roger Prong of Orgasm Research Foundation. And Miss Tarantella Serpentine. And you know Stella."

"I'll say he does," Stella agreed ambiguously. "Dr. Prong, it's an honor, a real honor. Ladies," Sput said with a vague half-gallant motion suggesting that he had almost risen. "Pull up a pillow and sit down. Take off your clothes if you want. Grab a hose from the hookah – or call one of the Pussiettes for a drink. My home is yours," he added grandly, making an Arabic gesture from an old Ronald Coleman movie. He was, Dill could see, stoned out of his gourd. As usual, the "Turkish tobacco" had made him philosophical.

They all sat down, and Dill motioned over a Pussiette to take their drink orders. Out of the corner of his eye, he saw Dr. Prong experimentally lifting the hookah hose to his lips. The doctor coughed, flushed with embarrassment, and sucked again.

"It's quite strong," he said thoughtfully.

Sput misunderstood, "Nothing but the best for my guests," he said grandly. "Fifty bucks an ounce."

The doctor looked amazed. "That's quite expensive for tobacco," he said, visibly impressed.

Sput stared at him, then grinned. "Quite a sense of humor you've got, Doc," he said jovially.

The doctor looked puzzled, then took another toke.

"Where's the swimming pool?" Tarantella asked.

"Through that door and downstairs," Sput said. "But it's full of noisy drunks right now, I think."

Stella, who had been toking very deeply, laid down the hose and closed both nostrils with her fingers. The doctor stared as she opened one and exhaled – for nearly twenty seconds. Then she inhaled for an equal length of time and closed both nostrils with her fingers again.

"What is that girl doing?" he asked Dill, apprehensively.

"Pranayama. A Hindu breathing exercise." Dill winked. "It often adds to the enjoyment of – Turkish tobacco."

"I'm going to take a swim," Tarentella announced. "Anybody want to come along?"

"Later," Dill said. "I'm just going to relax here for a while." He took another enormous toke.

"When I started *Pussycat*," Sput announced suddenly, returning to his previous mood and topic, "I had only one thought in mind: increasing the total amount of freedom in the world. Of course," he added with a roguish grin, "it wasn't against my principle to get rich in the process. But freedom was paramount. And now, after twenty years, what do I see? What do I see? I'll tell you what I see. People are as shit-scared and cowardly as ever, and still waiting for orders. Nothing can change humanity. Jesus couldn't do it. Jefferson couldn't do it. Even *I* can't do it. People are hopeless."

"You worry too much," Stella said sympathetically. "About people. And freedom. And all that shit."

Sput stared at her suddenly, "Stella," he said. "The lady with no last name. I am bored, Stella. I am uneasy and suffering from existential *angst* and several other fashionable varieties of heebie-jeebies, I am dying, Egypt, dying. Everybody is waiting for me to live up to my reputation. Would you give me a blow job? Right here? Right now?"

"I was wondering when you'd ask," she said. "You personally introduce me to three Hollywood producers afterwards, agreed?"

"Four. I'm in a generous mood."

"Done," she said, scuttling forward to grapple with his fly.

"Does this tobacco have a *drug* in it?" Dr. Prong asked suspiciously. "I'm feeling very strange suddenly."

"Hey," a woman yelled. "Sput's about to get a blow job." A small crowd began to gather.

"Wait," Sput said, as his trousers were pulled down. "You've got to say something first."

"What is it?" Stella asked, obviously amused by his fantasies.

"You say: 'I'm Mary Poppins, and I want to suck you off, Sput.' And, uh, 'I want your white hot come gushing into my mouth.' "

"Okay. I'm Mary Poppins and I want to suck you off, Sput, I want your white hot come gushing into my mouth."

"With conviction, damn it. *With conviction!*"

"There must be a drug in this stuff," Dr. Prong said. "I can *feel* it. I really ought to leave." He made no move to stand up. He looked about him, somewhat vaguely, and saw Sput, stripped from the waist down, his cock vanishing into Stella's mouth. "Oh, Jesus," he muttered. "It must be a hallucinogen. Not even the publisher of *Pussycat* would be doing that in a room full of people." He squinted thoughtfully. "Miss Only – I mean, Stella – am I imagining this?"

"Glub, glub," was the answer.

"Mr. Dill, am I imagining this?"

"Have another toke, Doc. The night is young." Dill had been whispering with a very attractive Pussiette and was now slipping his own trousers down.

Dr. Prong wasn't listening. He had become absorbed in one of the pillows. "What an amazing shade of blue," he was saying to nobody in particular. "Must be two threads very cleverly woven together.”

“Hike yourself around this way,” Dill was telling the Pussiette. “I want to sixty-nine.”

“Swallow it, swallow it all, Mary Poppins,” Dr. Prong heard a voice crying, “swallow every goddamn drop, *you bloody English snob*. I AM AN AMERICAN!”

“I have fallen out of reality into fantasy,” Dr. Prong said thoughtfully.

Behind him a stereo began to blare Buffy Saint Marie:

“God is alive, magic is afoot. . .”

CHAPTER EIGHT

Is there Life after Death?

Thirty blocks west of the bash at Sput's pad a certain Mr. Stanislaus Oedipusky was watching television with his fiancée, Miss Mary Kelly.

"Right, right!" the emcee was shouting hysterically, as if announcing the first contact with an extraterrestrial intelligence. "You have just won $27,000. Now do you want to try for $81,000?"

Stanislous yawned cavernously. "Wanna try the movies?" he asked. *King Kong* is on Channel 9 again."

"No, no," Miss Kelly said. "This is exciting."

Stan sighed. He hated the show they were watching because it confused him. *Prove Your Conspiracy* was the rage of the TV season, but it was perhaps a bit too tricky for Ma and Pa in the living room there in Des Moines and certainly wouldn't get renewed next year. The contestants were ordinary men and women who had devoted themselves, like many Kennedy assassination buffs, to unearthing complex and far-reaching conspiracies in or out of government. A panel of experts consisting of a young Harvard professor with enough good looks to be unintimidating, a popular Broadway columnist, and a famous retired Hollywood cowboy who set trick questions about facts that wouldn't fit the contestant's conspiracy theory. The contestant then had to explain the facts, or at least explain them away.

Tonight's contestant was a believer in the Bavarian Illuminati, a secret society of bankers, Satanists and communists who had allegedly controlled the world since 1776.

Stanislaus Oedipuski disliked the show because he could never make up his mind whether or not the conspiracies discussed were *really* real.

Besides, he had certain plans tonight for Miss Kelly – her parents were away for two days – and *King Kong* was definitely more erotic than all this palaver about Bavarian commies and devil-worshippers switching a Carcano-Mannlicher for Oswald's own rifle and hypnotizing Sirhan Sirhan by remote control.

"I'll try for $81,000," the contestant – a balding accountant from the Bronx – said gamely.

"Goodness, this is exciting," Mary Kelly bubbled enthusiastically.

"Yeah," Stan said, opening another can of beer.

"We'll be back with your question right after this word from our sponsor," the emcee cried as if announcing the second coming of Christ.

On the screen came an incredible girl – far lovelier than Monroe or Dietrich in their primes – hanging up a phone and looking morose and despondent. "Good grief," she said into the camera, "that's the third time he's been 'too busy' for a date." She frowned in perplexity. "Is there something wrong with me?"

Stan casually let his hand rest on Miss Kelly's shoulder and gave an affectionate, brotherly squeeze. On the screen an actor appeared wearing a costume consisting of two nostrils beneath which only his lower legs could be seen. "POST-NASAL DRIP," he thundered through an echo chamber. The camera panned in for a quick close-up on the actress, looking guilty and trapped. "Good grief," she cried with girlish anguish. "Could *I* have post-nasal drip?" The scene cut to a row of actors, all dressed in nose costumes and dancing as they sang a song about the perils of post-nasal drip. Another actor appeared, wearing a white smock (below him on the screen was the caption, A DRAMATIZATION); "Doctors know . . ." he began with an earnest frown.

Stan moved his hand slightly and felt the side of Miss Kelly's breast. His face was blank, absorbed in the actor talking about sinus-passage congestion; it almost seemed that his hand was acting without his awareness. Miss Kelly quietly reached up and pushed it back to her shoulder. The dancing noses were back, singing about the sponsor's product; and in twenty seconds the hand was back again, resting in the most friendly fashion possible against her breast. "No," she said, pushing it away.

Now on the screen a housewife was staring with bugged eyes out at the audience. "A cock in my kitchen!" she cried with great astonishment. The camera, in a zoom shot, picked up a rooster standing on the sink behind her. The rooster threw back its head and crowed, then miraculously turned into a cartoon rooster on a box of Chanticleer (IT MAKES *EVERYTHING* CLEAN) Suds. "Yes," an invisible announcer shouted "be cleaner than clean – and have a cock in *your* kitchen!" Miss Kelly giggled nervously and pushed away the hand again although it seemed to have wandered back as quietly as a shy puppy.

"We're gonna get married," Stan said mournfully, still staring at the screen.

"We're not married yet," Miss Kelly said primly.

The hand dangled hopelessly, like a wounded soldier. Then, by some strange navigation that she didn't see, it arrived suddenly in her lap, where it collapsed as if dead and totally harmless.

"No," she said, and the hand crept away like a dying kitten. But now he was kissing her ear.

"Honestly," she said, exasperated, "you only think of *one thing*."

"I love you," he breathed mournfully.

"Then you'd respect me," she said sharply.

He kissed her again. "Even the priest wouldn't say an engaged man shouldn't kiss his fiancée." He sighed again, profoundly. "Sometimes I think you don't love me at all."

"YES," A cowboy was shouting from the screen, "WE WANT REAL ROUGH TOUGH HE-MAN'S UNDIES OUT HERE IN THE WEST. WE WANT JOCKEY JOE JOCKIE SHORTS." The picture cut to a close-up of the crotch area of a dummy wearing Jockey Joe Jockie Shorts, with a convincing bulge in the appropriate place. Miss Kelly giggled again, more nervously than before. "You don't love me at all," Stan was plaintively rumbling, while his mouth traced an affectionate path from her earlobe to the corner of her mouth.

"I do love you," she said, "and I do want to marry you. But I want you to be proud of me. I don't want you to think I'm just another tramp like Nancy Gibbons."

"I love you, too," Stan spoke as if from his deathbed. "I love you so much it hurts." The hand was in her armpit, quite still, not approaching the breasts at all. "I love you and respect you. Honest!" The hand crept a centimeter further and stopped. "Just one kiss," she said boyishly, "and then we'll watch the TV."

"GROIN ODOR CAN BE OFFENSIVE," the announcer shouted. "That's why Jockey Joe Jockie Shorts come equipped with a built-in deodorant pad of clean, clean white cotton . . .

"Just one kiss," Miss Kelly said judiciously. "Just one."

A passing car cast its headlights upon their window. Its radio blared at them:

> "God is alive,
>
> Magic is afoot . . ."

"Just one," Mary repeated firmly.

CHAPTER NINE

How many angels can dance on the head of a pin?

Markoff Chaney, feeling like a perfect damned fool but excited nonetheless, padded down a hall wearing a Teddy Snowcrop suit. The third door, the butler had told him, was the bedroom where his hostess awaited him.

"Insanity is the only viable alternative," he repeated to himself. Then he pushed the door open and entered the first rich people's bedroom he had ever seen.

There was, as he had been told, only one light, behind the bed, playing upward on the ceiling and shedding a soft glow by reflection. The bed was made up, covered with an expensive-looking heirloom spread. Beside it, lit up nicely by the indirect light, was the table bearing a single can of Snowcrop orange juice, as he had expected.

And on the bed, nude, eyes tightly closed and pretending to sleep, was his hostess.

Chaney caught his breath. Judging from what he was expected to do, he had been prepared to see a crazy old frump; instead, to his intense delight, it was obvious that the lady was still fairly young, quite well preserved and definitely *stacked*. Crazy she might be (but how could he judge? Maybe it was normal for rich people to act out any fantasy that struck them) but unappetizing she definitely was not.

Although she was the first naked woman he had ever seen alive, outside of his magazines and Tarot cards, she was not a disappointment and not strikingly less golden and rounded

than, say, the *Pussycat* Sex Kitten of the Month. A head of
gloriously fiery red hair was spread on the pillow, and below
it her pretendedly sleeping face was lovely in its peaceful
anticipation. His eyes swept over her rounded shoulders, the
two snowy-white breasts rising and falling with her respiration,
the cute nipples that stood in surprisingly large aureoles upon
those breasts, the soft pillow of her belly, and, best of all, the
thick swatch of reddish fur that hid her sex. And she had legs
like a chorus girl.

He felt himself becoming erect at the very sight of her. My
first woman, he thought, at last. His mouth was dry and his
heart began to pound. He stood frozen, breathing a prayer
of gratitude, hardly able to believe that this was reality, not
fantasy.

She's waiting for me. For *me*.

Markoff Chaney experienced true happiness. Boldly,
he stepped forward and grabbed the orange juice can. An
opener lay beside it and he quickly punched two holes, his
hands trembling a bit – when the lady's belly moved with her
breathing, he felt his penis stir in the same rhythm.

Then, clutching the juice can in one hand, he hoisted himself
onto the bed, catching her in a sudden smile. But she was good
at the game: her eyes still didn't open.

Carefully, he lay beside her hip, looking at those breasts,
those real female breasts, not in a photograph but right there in
bed with him. Then, with infinite delicacy, he lifted the can and
let some of the orange juice dribble onto her bush.

She sighed and a tremor ran through her.

He poured a little more, and her legs spread voluptuously
and she slowly raised her knees. He was seeing it at last, the
outer lips and the cleft revealed as he had always dreamed of it,
the halo of reddish fur even more lovely than his fantasies. He
dribbled some more orange juice and leaned over, pushing the
snout onto her bush and maneuvering his tongue into the cleft
between the lips.

She was delicious. His head swam: in all his fantasies, he
had never imagined a woman's sexual flow mixed with orange
juice, and it was superb. He licked up and down between the
lips, trembling at the flavor and the rapidly increasing heat of
her. The lips were swelling and he felt the inner lips at last,
becoming thick with passion also. He quickly poured in some
more orange juice and went blindly hunting for her clitoris with
his tongue. He found it – a delightfully pert little button – and
took it between his lips. Immediately, she groaned and threw
her legs over his shoulders, pulling him own deeper into her
crotch. "Teddy," she murmured, "you've come back."

We all live in our fantasy and only endure our reality, he
thought philosophically. According to instructions, he began
a spiral licking motion, working from the outer lips slowly
inward around the inner lips and ending with the clitoris again.
She began to heave up and down as if being fucked, and
his excitement grew, as he imagined and participated in her
sensations.

Her hands were on the ears of his Teddy Snowcrop costume
and she was pulling him down onto her frantically as she
bucked upwards literally fucking his mouth with her cunt. He
began lapping her more rapidly, quite distinctly tasting the
musty female-in-passion flavor mixed with orange juice. Any
bar that dared to serve this – the Come Cocktail, it might be
called – would do a land-office business, before the police
closed them down. He pictured the kitchen where some lucky
soul would rub the women off into the orange juice; Christ,
what an idea.

"Oh, your tongue, your tongue," she cried. "In me, Teddy, in
me."

The midget maneuvered his tongue into her vagina and
bobbed his head in imitation fucking motions. Her legs went
limp on his back, then tight, then limp again. She's close to
coming, he thought rapturously. I'm making a woman come at
last. He strained, sticking his tongue further into her, maddened

by the thicker and heavier taste of her and losing the orange juice can entirely in his passion. He got both hands under her and lifted her ass, drawing her pussy up to him, sucking desperately as he plunged his tongue again and again deeper and deeper into her.

"TEDDY SNOWCROP!" she screamed insanely. "FRODO BAGGINS!! PETER PAN!!! CHILDHOOD!!!! INNOCENCE!!!! EAT MY PUSSY!!!!" She was coming, gushing like an oil well, all the female juices of her flowing into his mouth, and he nibbled the outer lips with his teeth, eyes tightly closed, riding on her cunt like a man hanging onto the edge of a cliff by his jaw muscles alone, bucking and bouncing with her, swallowing the essence of her womanhood. And now after decades and decades of frustration, finally coming, exploding from the sheer lust of her soul communicated to him in every spasm and twitch of her passionate pussy.

He thought two things: Now they're going to have to clean the Teddy Snowcrop suit.

And: I wonder if I'm still technically a virgin.

CHAPTER TEN

Who is the Master who makes the grass green?

"Do what thou wilt shall be the whole of the law," intoned Simeon Luna.

"What is thy will?" responded Little Sister Teresa.

"To eat and drink," he intoned.

"For what purpose?" she asked again.

"To replenish my body," he responded ritually.

"For what purpose?"

"To carry on the Great Work."

"Fall to!" she exclaimed. "Love is the law, love under will."

And so dinner began at the First Church of Scientific Illuminism.

"What is the agenda for tonight?" asked Brother Mordecai, forking a shrimp and dunking it in a sauce of catsup, horse radish and peyote shreddings.

"I have to trace down those Super Vibes we've all been noticing," Simeon Luna replied, digging into the lobster-in-hashish-supreme.

"Do you have any fix on it?" asked Sister Kteis, taking a snort of cocaine.

"Oh, yes," Simeon Luna answered easily. "It's somewhere to the South. In Chicago. North of the Loop. Around the Gold Coast probably." He sliced a piece of filet mignon.

"Is it Neg-ESP or just static?" Brother Fang the Unwashed asked curiously.

"It's a *Mama Vibe*," Simeon Luna said, sounding awed. "Some lonely soul who has turned on totally and doesn't even know what he's doing."

"That could be dangerous," Little Sister Teresa commented dubiously.

" 'Fear is failure,' " Simeon quoted. " 'No spell or scourge can harm those who have righteousness as their armor.' " He dipped his cup into the punch bowl, which contained 150-year-old cognac slightly spiked with psilocybin.

And so the Illuminati feasted and plotted, while the *Mama Vibe* continued to radiate . . .

Stanislaus Oedipusky had the hand back on Mary's shoulder again and sunk the thumb into an armpit.

"What I want to know," the Harvard professor on the TV was asking, "is this: if the Illuminati covered up all the evidence on the Kennedy assassinations, and the King assassination, and the wreck of the *Titanic* – as you say – and have buried all those fake fossils to make us think the world is older than 4000 years and lead us to doubt the Bible, why in heaven's name haven't they killed you yet? When this is your third week on this show?"

The camera panned in on a tight close-up of the contestant, a balding man with a haggard and nervous expression.

"They dare not kill me," he began, "because of Certain Papers I have placed in a sealed bank vault. Stories from *The New Yorker* with every fifth word underlined, showing how they communicate with each other right out in the open – and people think those stories don't mean anything, *hah!* – and old Fulton Sheen columns, with every third word underlined, and . . ."

Stan was perplexed. He wished to hell he could decide whether the Illuminati really existed or not. Meanwhile, he slowly eased the hand down into the armpit, to join the thumb.

"No," Mary said promptly.

"I'm not *touching* you," Stan cried, feeling unjustly accused. "I'm not *touching* you!"

"Well, you're not touching me in a *bad* place, but you're starting again . . ."

"What's wrong with an armpit? *Just because it's hairy?*" Stan asked, ungrammatically but very sincerely.

Mary looked temporarily puzzled, and the ex-cowboy panelist asked, "Is there anybody you can name who *isn't* part of the Illuminati?"

"Well, Spiro Agnew probably . . ." the contestant began.

Dinner at the First Church of Scientific Illuminism was completed and Simeon Luna had retired to his sacristy to seek astral contact with the *Mama Vibe*. Little Sister Teresa assisted him.

Simeon lay on the floor, nude, in the position of the Hanged Man from the Tarot deck. He chanted the most powerful Name in all magick, IAO, the sound that is capable of any desired effect *if* one knows how to pronounce it, which is why no textbook on the occult ever dares to give the pronunciation. (Hint: it has three syllables.)

"IAO, IAO, IAO," Simeon chanted. "Thou Great Wild Beast, IAO, IAO, IAO, Goat of Mendes, IAO, IAO, IAO, IAO, *Panphage meta Pangenitor,* IAO, IAO, IAO, IAO, IAO, IAO . . ."

Sister Teresa, eyes tightly closed, sucked very slowly up and down Simeon's penis. In her mind, both his and her body had slowly faded away; all that existed was the penis, filling all space, and she was all starry energy surrounding it. In Simeon's mind, he *was* IAO, *was* the penis, *was* all matter and existence. In short, together they were in *Kether*, the topmost reach of the Astral World.

"IAO, IAO, IAO, IAO, IAO," the chant continued.

Looking down at *Malkuth* (our material world) from *Kether*, in the astral realm, Simeon began to find the *Mama Vibe* . . .

CHAPTER ELEVEN

Where do these questions come from?

CHINA, 700 A. D.: A perplexed young man came to the Master Ped Xing, foremost exponent of Ch'an Buddhism, the most radical of all Buddhist sects. "Master," said the young man, "I seek illumination."

"How can you seek illumination," replied old Xing, "when you already own the light of the universe?"

"How do I own the light of the universe?" asked the young man, more perplexed than when he had entered.

"Where does that question come from?" Ped Xing asked.

AFGHANISTAN, 1100 A. D.: Hassan i Sabbah, the Old Man of the Mountains, Grandmaster of the Assassins, Lord of the Brothers of Light, prophet of the Ismaelian sect of Islam, first in a long line of Aga Khans, was in addition to these accomplishments the inventor of the time-release capsule, which he was careful to keep secret.

Looking down upon two young men who had just finished eating dinner with him, the noble Lord Hassan said, "Take them to the garden."

Servants were quick to obey, and the young men – being sound asleep – did not object. The time-release capsule in their food had released a heavy dose of opium and they were quite thoroughly unconscious and unaware of their surroundings.

The garden – officially known as "the Garden of Delights" – covered several acres. Here candidates were prepared for admission to the Order of the Assassins: they were to become the most feared and legendary professional killers in history. But here also, in this same garden, were prepared candidates for admission to the Brotherhood of Light, the Illuminati. The candidates, in fact, were prepared the same way. They themselves selected, unknown to themselves, which order they would enter – the political Assassins or the mystic Illuminati.

Both young men were conveyed into the Garden of Delights and placed several acres apart from each other. In a short time, the second stage of the time-release capsule began to work; cocaine was released into their bloodstreams, thereby overwhelming the traces of the soporific opium and causing them to awaken full of energy and zest. At the same time, as they woke, hashish also began to be released, so they saw everything with exceptional clarity and all colors were jewel-like, brilliant, divinely beautiful.

A group of extremely beautiful young ladies – imported from the most expensive brothel in Cairo – sat in a circle around each of the young candidates, playing upon lutes and other delicately sweet Oriental musical instruments. "Welcome to heaven," they sang as the awakening men gazed about them in wonder. "By the magic of the holy Lord Hassan, you have entered Paradise while still alive." And they fed them "paradise apples" (oranges), far sweeter and stranger than the earth-apples they had known before, and they showed them the animals of paradise (imported from as far away as Japan, in some cases), creatures far more remarkable than those ordinarily seen in Afghanistan.

"This *is* heaven!" the first young man exclaimed, in ecstasy. "Great is Allah, and great is the wise Lord Hassan-i Sabbah!"

But, twenty acres away, surrounded by similar lovely ladies and other wonders, the second young man merely gazed about him, smiled in contentment, and said nothing.

And then, in both cases, the *houris* of Paradise, as promised in the *Koran*, began to dance, and as they danced, they discarded one by one each of their seven veils. As the veils were thrown off, more and more hashish was released from the capsules and the young men saw with greater clarity, felt with deeper intensity, experienced beauty and sexual joy in a way completely unknown in their previous earth lives.

Then, as each young man sat entranced by the beauty and wonder of Heaven, the *houris* finished the dance, and nude and splendid as they were, rushed forward in a bunch, like flowers cast before the wind. And some fell at the candidate's feet and kissed his ankles; some kissed knees or thighs, one sucked raptly at his penis, others kissed the chest and arms and belly, a few kissed eyes and mouth and ears. And as he was smothered in this hashish-intensified avalanche of love, the lady working on his penis sucked and sucked and sucked until he came in her mouth as softly and slowly and blissfully as a single snowflake falling.

In a little while, there was no more hashish being released and more opium began to flow into the bloodstream. The young candidates slept again; and in their torpor, they were removed from the Garden of Delights and returned to the banquet hall of the Lord Hassan.

There they awoke.

"Truly," the first exclaimed, "I have seen the glories of Heaven, as foretold in the blessed *Al Koran*. I have no more doubts. I will trust Hassan i Sabbah and love him and serve him, more than ever did I trust or love or serve mine own father."

"You are accepted for the Order of Assassins," said the gracious Lord Hassan, grave and solemn.

"Go at once to the Green Room to meet your superior in the Order."

When this candidate had left, Hassan turned to the second, asking, "And you?"

"I have discovered the greatest treasure in the universe," he said simply, "and it is my own mind."

Hassan i Sabbah grinned broadly. "Welcome to the Order of the Illuminati!" he said, laughing.

BAVARIA, 1780 A. D.: In the legend-haunted old town of Ingolstadt, three doors from the house where young Victor von Frankenstein pursued research that was to make his name infamous, Adam Weishaupt, Grand Primus *Illuminatus* of the Bavarian Illuminati, 33° Free and Accepted Mason, 10° Order of Oriental Templars, first speaker of the Grand Orient Lodge of Reformed (Cagliostroan) French Freemasons, and professor of Canon Law at the University of Ingolstadt, worked late at night, finishing his horrible treatise *Uber Strip Schnipp-Schnapp, Weltspielen und Funfwissenschaft,* which future generations were to classify with Ludvig Prinn's *De Vermis Mysteriis* and mad Abdul Alhazred's feared *Necronomicon* as one of the three most terrible books in the whole world.

"Truly," Professor Weishaupt was writing, "few men have shown such exemplary and grandmotherly kindness as the noble Hassan i Sabbah, whose assassinations, by striking only at public figures, prevented any necessity to send an army into combat. Here we see the pragmatic equivalent of sentimental pacifism united with the moral alternative to war, all in one neat package. It was with simple truth that Abdul Alhazred wrote of Sabbah, 'This was an Illuminated Mind.' And yet, we in our scientific eighteenth century must not rest on of Sabbah's teachings; we must advance *one step further –*"

He stopped writing because he was laughing too loud to hold the pen in his hand. The candle flame wobbled as his guffaws exploded upward from his belly, and strange lights danced upon the walls. The laughter continued, bounced around the room, echoed onto the street outside.

A passing burgher heard and piously crossed himself, hurrying onward. It was well known that Adam Weishaupt was a deep one and Lord only knew what such fiendish laughter implied.

"It is time for the Illuminati to become scientific," Weishaupt scribbled on, still barely controlling his mirth. "And for this end, we shall go underground for two hundred years. And then . . ."

The fiendish sound of his laughter woke the cat, Robin, who prudently leaped out the window and kept running until he reached Munich.

CHAPTER TWELVE

Is God male? female? or neuter?

Back at Sput's pad things were also getting a bit spooky.

Dr. Prong sat amid a wall-to-wall sea of writhing, panting, gasping bodies. He was seeing various mathematical curves made by the rise and fall of shoulders, legs, hips and various other parts; and he was quite happily trying to remember the names and equations for each curve. He was very definitely stoned although imperfectly aware of the fact.

"You lonely?" a Pussiette asked, crawling toward him.

"Not at all," he said. "I thought I was under the influence of some drug for a while, but obviously I'm not. In fact, I'm thinking with quite remarkable clarity."

"Oh, boy, yeah," she said. "You're too stoned to join the fun."

"Young lady, believe me, you're quite mistaken. Religion, mathematics and sex are all the same. I just discovered that." Dr. Prong stared at her owlishly. "A drugged man does not do mathematics," he added.

Tarantella Serpentine, who had evidently returned from the pool a while back, crawled over. "Oh, yeah, baby," she said. "You're not drugged at all. But now you're going to give me the treatment I always give you."

And with no other word than that, the brazen girl sunk onto her back and dragged his head down into her crotch.

"Oh, really," he said, "not in public, like this. These people are all drugged and unscrupulous. I'm sure."

"Encourage him, honey," Tarantella said impishly to the Pussiette.

Without a word, the other girl, equally devoid of any sense of the fitness of things, began undoing his belt.

"Now just a damn minute – " Dr. Prong started to protest. But she went right ahead and in a minute her tongue was flicking up and down his wand with fiery little flashes. Meanwhile, Tarantella had both hands on his head and was pulling it between her legs.

"I really don't – glub, glub," he said, still not quite believing all this.

But the tongue on his tool was carrying him to a point where he was not able to argue with anybody. Obediently, he began placing little kisses on Tarentella's bush, thinking of the pleasure she had given him that afternoon. Meanwhile, the tongue had stopped its up-and-down passage and was monotonously and insistently circling the rim of his cockhead, building up a charge in him that was quite surprising, considering his very recent orgasm.

A sudden motion to the right drew his eyes. Sput was standing up, leaning forward over a girl who kneeled on hands and knees before him, taking his penis into her rectum. Another man, standing before her, was dreamily jacking off, and she had her mouth open, watching, waiting to catch his come on her tongue when he climaxed.

Too bad I can't take notes, Dr. Prong thought, how the other half lives. But Tarantella's musky bush, pushing up against his mouth and nose, was now quite wet and he reminded himself to continue licking it, while the darling girl at his port was now gobbling his prick quite intensely. He looked down to see if she was getting any direct stimulation and saw that a third girl had joined their daisy chain and was licking each breast alternately, while Dill busily sucked at *her* snatch and kept one finger in the Pussiette's heaving twat. It was all very cozy, but Dr. Prong wondered if that damn drug had loused up everybody's sense

     The Sex Magicians

of decorum.

It would be a *mathematical miracle* if we all come at once, he thought.

The Pussiette, meanwhile, was quite conscious that the lips on her nipples were female, but that somewhat queer note didn't disturb her; rather, it added to the general excitement. The finger in her honey-box must have been male, and the cock in her mouth definitely was, and she reached out one caressing hand to the breasts of the girl who was sucking on her, while feeling Dr. Prong's prong suddenly get hotter and harder in her mouth, and she suddenly had a flash of thinking group ecstasy reverberating by chain reaction from one to another must be what heaven was like, but then the hot salty spash on her tongue catapulted her into ecstasy and Dill moved his finger carefully inside her to help her along and the other girl nibbled very gently on her nipples and she went completely out of herself in spasm after spasm.

And even Dr. Prong had quite forgotten about the sinister machinations of Ezra Pound and the Fair Play for Fernando Poo Committee.

Chapter Thirteen

Who knows what Evil lurks in the hearts of men?

Things were somewhat more restrained at the Kelly household.

Well after an hour of importuning, Stan had gotten the hand under Mary's sweater, to rest on the brassiere, but he was still under strict taboo not to move it very much, and especially not to move it during the open-mouth kisses.

Those kisses, however, were proceeding nicely. Mary Kelly was definitely breathing hard and sometimes when she said "no" again neither he nor she was quite sure what exactly she was forbidding.

"DON'T LET ATHLETE'S FOOT RUIN YOUR MARRIAGE," the TV was blaring. "NINE OUT OF TEN DOCTORS SAY –"

"We should really stop," Mary gasped.

"I can't stop," Stan moaned. "You have awakened the tiger in me." He kissed her again, impassionedly, and dared to feel around for the nipple at the same time. To his delight it was definitely becoming perceptible under the bra.

"No, please, don't do that," Mary breathed. But this time she made no move to stop him, Indeed her hands were clenched into little fists as if she were fighting not him but herself.

"I love you, I love you," he gasped, like a whale cast up on a beach, meanwhile working the nipple something fierce.

"Puh-*lease*," she said, but her little fists were still as unresisting as dead soldiers.

　　　　　　　　　　　　　　　　　　The Sex Magicians

Stan gamely dropped a hand into her lap again – a tactical mistake, it turned out, for she went rigid at once and put both fists on his chest, pushing him away. "NO," she howled, in the voice of one undergoing an exquisite Chinese torture.

Stan retreated. "I'm sorry," he muttered like a thief caught in the act. "You get me so worked up –"

"We better stop," she said. "Before I get you more worked up."

"Just one more kiss," Stan begged pathetically.

"No, we shouldn't –"

"I won't touch you again. Honest."

"We really shouldn't –"

"POST KRISPIES," the TV roared, "WILL GIVE YOUR LITTLE SPACE RANGER A TASTY AND NUTRITIOUS BLAST-OFF EVERY MORNING." A penile-shaped rocket was seen racing toward the moon.

Neither Stan nor Mary saw it. They were lost in what she thought of as a passionate soul-kiss. She was counting mentally because a local expert on morality had told her that it became sinful after twenty seconds. Alas, she lost count around fourteen.

Back at Orgasm Research, a pre-med student named Marvin Gardens had long since replaced the psych student. On his own authority, because he had become curious about the direction of this experiment, he had brought in the necessary equipment to begin feeding Josie intravenously. Marvin himself was munching an apple and taking an occasional note.

Josie was bathed in sweat. The feeding equipment was plugged into her left arm, the ACE equipment hovered above her like some sinister interplanetary robot, and the bottom sheets were twisted and torn in a few places as if bears had been sleeping in the bed. Her eyes were entirely out of focus whenever she opened them and she was speaking her fantasies in the dead-level schizzy tone of a narco-analysis patient: "You coon," she was saying, "you big black buck. Give it to me. Ram it into me. I wanna come again. Make me come again . . ."

King Kong dutifully plugged away at her raw and cavernous pussy.

Marvin Gardens made a note, munching his apple, unaffected by her moans and spasms. He was a homosexual.

"I could weep when I think of my fellow countrymen," Sput said, toking again on the hookah. "They started with the greatest Constitution in the history of the world and have spent nearly two hundred years twisting it backwards to allow themselves the masochistic pleasure of being victimized by tyrants. Separation of church and state, the constitution says – and they've fastened on their own backs a priestly tyranny so archaic that any visiting Englishman or Frenchman thinks he's fallen through a time warp back into the Middle Ages. No laws restricting freedom of the press, the constitution says – and there isn't a single media from TV to deaf-and-dumb sign language that isn't policed, regulated, censored, bowdlerized, controlled, restricted, castrated. No wars without the consent of congress, the constitution says – and they let any dimwit in the White House invade any country from here to Fernando Poo, and don't have balls enough to start impeachment proceedings. They're even giving up their right to bear arms. And the fact that they're spied on every time they pick up a phone – the fact that they can't even take a crap in a public john without some creep from the vice squad watching them through a peep hole to make sure they don't do anything faggotty – the fact that they have less privacy than the Germans under Hitler – doesn't bother them a whit. They just sprawl there with the faces in the mud and their butts in the air, wiggling and saying 'Stick it into me again, just like you did before.' And the bureaucrats in Washington are glad to oblige. I tell you," he added morosely, "it's enough to make a grown man weep.

"You worry too much," Stella said sympathetically. "You're all heart, Sput."

Stan Oedipusky was making more progress. His hand was under Mary's skirt, pressing gently against the crotch of her panties.

"Please," Mary was saying, almost in agony, "Please, Stan . . ." It wasn't too clear what she was asking for, and he covered her lips in another kiss before she could express herself in more detail.

Unfortunately, he had to break for a breath of air, and she had a chance to speak again. "I can't," she panted, wild-eyed, looking in general like the survivor of a bombed-out city. "I'm *afraid*, Stan!"

"I won't hurt you," he gasped, easing a finger over the top of her panties. "Honest to God, Mary, I won't hurt you."

Josie stood on top of the Empire State Building, and this time the planes from Floyd Bennet Field were late in arriving. He hovered above her, growling and sniffing; they were alone at last, and his dark eyes blazed with his gross and brutal passion for her (for her!). Slowly his enormous whang began to swell – one foot, two feet, three feet. When it reached five incredible pulsating feet in length, he threw back his head and began to beat his chest, roaring his savage cry of passion into the sky.

At last, King Kong – free finally of censors, in the privacy of Josie's feverish mind – was taking his bride.

"Another thing that almost drives me to tears," said Sput philosophically, "is the custard-headed imbecility of the so-called opposition or counterculture in this perishing republic. Clowns who are trying to organize a mass rebellion, but insult the masses every time they open their mouths. Lame brains who oppose censorship here at home but find very elegant excuses to defend it anywhere else in the world. Idiots who cry out for liberty but are eager to accept any dictator who comes along. Epistemological illiterates who don't know the difference between an argument and an assertion. Clods with no more courtesy than the Jukes family, no more tolerance than the Ku Klux Klan, no more sophistication than Jeeter Lester, and no more humor than Cotten Mather. Why, if I pick one of them for an interview in my magazine, they spend half their space saying that I'm a pimp, a whoremonger, a slave owner, a pig and an imperialist – and when I show my own respect for freedom of the press by printing their incoherent gibberings, they sneer at me as an old-fashioned liberal. I could weep, I tell you, I could weep."

Beside him, Dill was busily and blearily spraying whipped cream from a can into Tarentella's crotch as she lay in total relaxation, nude and gleaming, on the floor. "Now, remember," she said, "if you want to do that, you've got to really do it, all the way. That stuff is sticky if it dries in. You've got to promise to lick all of it off, *all* of it."

"I promise," Dill said happily, "I promise already."

"And another thing," Sput went on, although nobody was listening, "the fat-headedness of contemporary science is almost as gross as that of the god-forsaken churches. Why, I remember a few years ago, when all those Buddhists were burning themselves to death to protest the American invasion of Vietnam; *Science News* did a survey to try to find out how they could sit so calm while blazing like torches. And who do you suppose they asked? A bunch of psychologists and neurologists – the last people in the world to know anything about it. (They don't even know yet that men kneel in churches because it gets their heads closer to the ground and makes them feel more like they've regressed to childhood.) If they knew anything about not feeling flame, they'd be able to *do* it, and they can't. They can't even bear the toothache patiently,

as a fellow named Shakespeare once said. But that's not the
final irony. The researchers didn't ask a single Buddhist. Not
one. It never occurred to them to ask the people who *can* do it.
What conceit! What occidental chauvinism! What pea-brained
fatuity. I could weep, I tell you."

"Zactly!" said Dr. Prong, sitting up suddenly and not noticing
how he jarred the neck of the lovely Pussiette who was sucking
him off at that moment. "We don't know any of the important
answers. We don't know what sensation is or what causes it
or what stops it. We don't know if the mind is in the brain or
spread all over the body, or even if it extends a few feet beyond
the body, like some of the Russian investigators think and all
the old mystics said. We don't know why people get turned on
to sex or art or good weather or anything, and we don't know
why they get turned off. And anybody who really tries to find
out gets thrown in jail, like Reich, or persecuted and driven to
an early grave, like Kinsey, or becomes an object of ridicule,
like me. And we stagger on in our ignorance, not knowing the
answers to any of the big questions."

"The *wig* questions," said Dill, getting to his knees,
his mouth smeared with whipped cream. "Think about
them enough and you blow your wig." He began to recite
portentously, "What is the sound of one hand clapping? Are
we all drinking the water or the wave? Who will guard the
guardians? Who knows what Evil lurks in the hearts of men?
Why is a duck?" He shook his head. "We'll never know," he
concluded profoundly, diving back into Tarentella's creamy
snatch.

"See?" said Sput. "I'm surrounded by Philistines."

But actually he was feeling quite happy. His mind had made
an abrupt leap and he suddenly saw the way to drive three of
his most dangerous competitors out of business.

"I never saw – one of them – before. Not when it was hard
I mean," said Mary Kelly, blushing prettily. "I mean, I only

saw my brother's once in the shower." She blushed again. The poor girl's heart was beating so fast that she could hardly hear anything else.

Stan squirmed, guiltily. "I'll love you forever for this. Honest I will. It's just that I can't wait no more. We been engaged three years already." He looked down at his penis, sticking up fat and bold out of his trouser fly, and he began to hear his own heart beating.

"Don't look at me," Mary said shyly. "Look over my head. Please."

"I will," he said humbly, with deep gratitude.

The girl took his penis in her fist and began rubbing it, noting with alarm that it was getting bigger and harder right away. After we're married, she thought, can I really take all that inside me? It didn't seem possible, but she knew that she wanted to try – as soon as they were married, of course. He just wouldn't respect her anymore, she knew, if she let him do it now.

Stan was watching some dancing cigars on the TV and vaguely, over the beating of his heart, he could hear them singing something about "you don't have to inhale to enjoy it." An actress appeared and took a cigar from an actor, sucking on it with suggestively flirtatious shivers of appreciation.

"Uh," he said, "Could you – could you – "

"What?" Mary asked. She was having trouble with her breathing: His cock seemed so hot and – alive – in her hand.

"Oh, nothing," he said, watching the actress purse her lips around the cigar again.

Mary went on rubbing him.

"Please," he said. "Let me look at you."

She blushed again. "I couldn't do that."

"Please."

"No, really! We should have the lights out. If my parents

came home unexpectedly, I'd just *die*."

"Let me touch you. Just touch you."

"No, Stan! I'm doing what you need. Don't get me in trouble."

"I won't put it in. Honest to God, I won't put it in. Just let me touch you – for a minute."

"Honestly! I feel guilty enough already." She began rubbing faster, trying to get it over with. Her own feelings betrayed her, though. She was trying not to look at what she was doing, but her eyes kept creeping back, and Stan's weapon now looked even bigger than it felt. For some odd reason, the size no longer frightened her, and she felt quite sure of her ability to take it all (after marriage, of course); she just *knew* she could take it – maybe because she suddenly felt very, well, loose and empty, down there.

Stan moaned. "Could you – could you – "

"What?"

"Oh, nothing." He was terrified to ask her; she would consider him a monster. Damn that actress and her big cigar.

"What are you going to – do it – on?" she asked suddenly, still rubbing.

He couldn't think. "The rug?"

"If my parents saw the stain, I'd *die*. I'd absolutely die."

"My handkerchief?"

"If your mother saw the stain, I'd *die*."

"The flower pot?"

"That's too close to the window. Somebody might see our shadows."

"For Christ's sake, I gotta come somewhere!"

"I know!" the girl said brightly. "In my *mouth*, and I can swallow it. Then nobody will ever, ever know. "

"Oh, yeah," Stan said weakly. "Why didn't I think of that?"

"Tell me when you're ready," she said in a strangled voice.

"NOW," he screamed. "NOW!"

Mary very delicately and nervously took the head between her lips, pulling her tongue way back in her mouth and making no further move.

"MORE," he said. "AN INCH MORE, PLLLLLLEASE!!!!!"

She took it out, and the sensation of her hand again almost made him think he'd spurt right into her ear. "Okay," she said bashfully, "but then you gotta be quick."

"I'll be quick, I'll be quick!" Stan's mouth was hanging loosely and his eyes were bugging out of his head.

"Well, then . . ." Mary took almost exactly a full inch and a half this time. Stan, catapulted into a dizzy rush of sensation, thrust two more inches into her mouth, his hands clutching desperately for her shoulders.

Suddenly he was thrusting into empty air. Her mouth had gone away.

"Goodness," she said nervously. "I'm glad that's over."

"OVER?" he screamed. "OVER? I didn't come yet!!"

Mary giggled shrilly. "Oh. Yes. I would have tasted it, I guess. I'm sorry, I just sort of blanked out, and I thought you were finished." She put her mouth back on his penis and began moving her lips rhythmically this time, taking three inches, then four . . .

"A titty," he whispered desperately. "Just let me see a titty."

"Mmmm, mmmm," she said, but the sound was affirmative. As he watched in astonished delight, she pulled her sweater up to her neck with both hands and began unhooking her bra, all without taking her mouth off his prick for a second. My God, she's got talent after all, he thought. The breasts hung bare, two cute nipples staring back at him. He groped, bending forward, and touched one. It was hard beneath his finger. He began thrusting blindly, holding the nipple between two fingers, ramming his cock further and further into her mouth, his eyes shut tight as he rode the waves of pleasure into a blackness and a sweetness that seemed to engulf him.

Then her mouth went away again.

"FOR JESUS SAKE," he bellowed, "WHAT IS IT THIS TIME?????!!"

The girl was staring at him out of a totally white face. "Put it in me," she mumbled, "I'll *die* if you don't put it in me."

Stan leaped off the couch, tearing his trousers down and almost tripping over them as she pulled her sweater the rest of the way off and began unzippering her skirt. In less than a minute he was sprawled on top of her on the floor, groping for the cleft between her lips.

"Let me," she said, guiding his prick into her. "All the way," she breathed, "All the way. No, don't move now, just hold it there all the way inside me. Oh, Jesus! Oh, Mary and Joseph! Oh, Sister Mary Agnes! Move it, move it!! *Double clutch* me, you mother fucker!!!"

Stan obligingly began thrusting as fast and as hard as he could. She was as wet and hot as if he had been fingering her pussy for twenty minutes, and her nails began to dig into his back as she strained upward to kiss him again and again. The nails dug into his buttocks, and she seemed to be trying to pull his whole pelvis into her. Her legs rose straight up in the air, then wrapped tightly; around his waist, and she began chanting like a demented priestess, "Oh, fuck, oh, fuck fuck, oh fuck fuck fuck fuck, fucky, fucky, fucky fuck fuck fuck, fucky fuck me, fuck me, fuckfuckfuckfuck . . ." He buried both hands in her hair, yanked her head backwards and kissed her as hard as he could, shoving his tongue far, far back in her mouth. Uck, uck, uck, uck me," she was chanting right through the kiss. Her virgin pussy, hungry with twenty-three years of frustration, seemed to pull on him with the same grip as her mouth, clutching and sucking on all seven inches of his penis. And when he stopped kissing to breathe she went on in

a new chant, "Cock, cock, I've got cock. I've got cock inside
me, Mother of God, I've got cock, cock, cock, cock, I've got
cock . . ." Her nails dug deep and hard into his butt, and he was
spurting into her, spurting again and again, and she screamed,
"In my pussy, in my pussy, in my pussy-pussy-pussy! " and she
bucked against him over and over and over and over until his
head swam.

Mary Kelly had left girl-hood behind.

The letterhead said FLAT EARTH RESEARCH SOCIETY
"In your heart you know it's flat" and beneath it he was typing
neatly:

The famous explorer F. Poo
Grew bored with the ocean so blue
His daily diversions
Were varied perversions
And he saved the night for a screw

He signed in a big round hand, "John Herbert Dillinger,"
folded it neatly, and slipped it in an envelope already addressed
to Dr. Roger Prong.

Markoff Chaney, out of the Teddy Snowcrop suit and
home at the Y, was ready to resume his crusade against the
mathematical mind.

Tarantella had gone exploring and found herself in a dimly lit
room where Stella and several other guys and gals were sitting
around naked with a punch bowl in the center of the floor. One
man, with a pointed beard and strange dark eyes, seemed to be
the center of attention.

"Remove your masks all players," he was chanting, "the
carnival draws to a close. Now we must stand spiritually as
well as physically naked."

"What's this?" Tarantella asked, sitting next to Stella.

"Take some of the Truth Serum first," Stella said. "It's Zen in

The Sex Magicians

the Art of Balling, dig?"

Tarentella tried some of the punch. There was no taste beyond papaya and pineapple, so she assumed that the mystery ingredient was probably LSD'

"You first," the bearded man said to Stella. "What's your most obsessive sexual fantasy?" "Well," she said, "it's silly."

"No dream of the human heart is silly," the bearded man said severely.

Stella, astonishingly, blushed. "Okay," she said, "I won't pussyfoot about it. I've always had this dream of an escalator, a mile long escalator, running past me and rising up to the sky. There are hundreds and hundreds of naked men on it. And as they pass me – well – well, I suck each one of them off. Hundreds and hundreds of them." She grinned awkwardly. "Like a dream of infinite cock, dig?" "Wow," another girl said, looking amazed.

"What about you?" the bearded man asked Dill. The editor shrugged. "I'm fairly corny, I guess. The only obsessive fantasy I have is a very old one. I'd like to dive head-first into a barrel of tits." He laughed, a bit too loud. "And, yeah, sometimes I change it. I'd like to roll naked, over and over, across an acre of tits." He laughed again.

"Don't be ashamed of it," the bearded man said. "It's your True Will. How about you?" he asked another girl.

"Oh," she said, "I've always had this thing where I'm lying naked in the middle of a swimming pool – an empty swimming pool, without water in it. And all around the top are men jacking off. But the nice thing is, they all come at once and every drop of sperm hits me at the same time and covers me from head to foot. Every inch of me." She tittered.

Another man spoke up. 'That's like my favorite fantasy," he said. "Except it's a coal mine instead of a swimming pool, and only one girl. I stand at the top of the shaft jerking my gherkin and she waits at the bottom with her mouth open to catch my sperm when I come." He stared into space. "God, the things that go on in our heads."

"I've got a man-jacking-off fantasy, too," another girl said thoughtfully. "But it's my father. He's always been very conservative and like proper, you know? I see him in a room all alone with my nude pictures that were in *Pussycat* and he's jacking off over them."

"And when he comes," Dill asked, laughing, "you rush in and confront him?"

"No," she said. "I don't want him to be embarrassed. I just want to watch through the peep hole and see with my own eyes that he's human, too."

"Out of *sight*." Stella said.

"I got one of those, too," a Jewish-looking man said with brooding introspection. "I mean not something I want to do, but something I want to see. Only it's not so personal." He smiled. "I'd like to see it on a stage, in a theater, with an audience of thousands of others beside myself. An orthodox rabbi eating a nun's pussy."

"They should do it during Brotherhood Week," Dill said, laughing.

"I had one for years," another girl said a bit wanly. "But it was too realistic – I wanted to have three guys at once. One with his cock in my mouth, one up my ass and one fucking me. I finally did it tonight, and now I don't have a fantasy anymore."

"You'll have a new one," the bearded man said. "Believe me: recent research has proven that people can't live without dreaming. If you wake them up every time they show rapid eye movements – which means that they're starting to dream – then they never finish a dream and they all get very sick very quickly. The same is true of waking fantasy."

"Are you a psychiatrist?" Tarantella asked him.

"No. I'm nothing like a psychiatrist," he replied with a

strange grin.

"You must be *something* like a psychiatrist," Stella objected. "I can tell."

"I'm in an older profession," he said simply. "And you," he said to Tarantella, "what's your fantasy?"

She shrugged. "I'm surprised every woman here hasn't mentioned it. It must be the most female of all fantasies. I want to lie naked on an altar in a church and have naked men kneel and worship me.

The bearded man looked at her thoughtfully. "That could happen, you know," he said mildly.

Mary Kelly was weeping. "You don't respect me anymore," she bawled. "I acted terrible, simply terrible."

Stan grimaced in anguish. "Oh, no. You acted *wonderful*. Honest. It was like a dream come true."

"You'll never want to marry me now," the girl sniffled.

"Yes, I will."

"No, you won't. I know what happens to girls who go all the way."

"Baby, I'll marry you as soon as possible." Stan couldn't stand her tears.

"No you won't."

"Yes I will."

"Next Sunday?"

Stan looked into the pit – but then in the pause, she started to weep again. "Yes," he said, leaping. "Next Sunday."

A bull rumbled across the TV screen and an announcer thundered, "MERRILL LYNCH IS BULLISH ABOUT AMERICA!"

CHAPTER FOURTEEN

What is outside the Universe?

"We're off to see the wizard," Stella was singing, "the wonderful Wizard of Oz . . .

Dr. Prong opened an eye and looked around. He seemed to be in a speeding automobile.

"Becuz, becuz, becuz, becuz," Josh Dill sang merrily.

"Becuz of the wonderful things he does," Stella finished. They both laughed.

"Where am I?" Dr. Prong asked, quite confused.

"Milky Way Galaxy," the driver said. He was a Satanic-looking chap with a black pointed beard. "Out near the rim," he added helpfully. "Third planet from a star whose correct name is IAO, also known as *Sol* or the *Sun*. On the plane of *Malkus*, in the eternal mind of *Brahm*. Got it?"

"We're in the clutches of the Bavarian Illuminati," Stella added. "You know, the gang that runs the whole world? The Great White Brotherhood."

"Great White Fuck-ups, I'd say," Tarantella Serpentine commented, "considering the shape the world is in."

"The world has no shape," Josh Dill interjected, vehemently. "Nothing has a shape."

Obviously, Dr. Prong thought, they were all being *mind warped* by some horrible hallucinogenic drug.

"Permit me to explain, Dr. Prong," the bearded driver said. "Unknown to yourself, you and these other people – and a few others we haven't located yet – are all part of a certain psychic experiment." "You're a scientist?" Dr. Prong asked dubiously. There was something about this fellow a bit too fey to fit the rigor of scientific discipline.

"In a sense. I'm also an ordained minister. In fact, I am, to be brief about it, the Reverend Doctor Simeon Luna of the First Church of Scientific Illuminism."

"Oh," Dr. Prong said noncommittally. To himself, he translated that title briefly as a *nut*.

The group now consisted of five people, three of whom thought three others were funny in the head.

"Ah, what is Scientific Illuminism?" Dr. Prong asked courteously, hiding his opinions.

Simeon Luna grinned. "I quote," he said:

We place no reliance
On virgin or pigeon
Our method is science
Our aim is religion

"Do what thou wilt shall be the whole of the law," he added.

That wasn't very helpful – and it vaguely reminded Dr. Prong of certain old secret societies of somewhat sinister reputation. "Where are we going?" he asked again.

"Evanston," said Simeon this time. "To our church. It's hidden, of course. Doesn't do to practice the rites of Isis out in the open. We'd have all the Christians, Jews and atheists in government down on us faster than you could say 'Abrahadabra.' No, we're well hidden: our coven meets in a secret basement beneath the basement of the Women's Christian Temperance Union. Last place anyone would think of looking for us."

"And can I ask why we're going to one of your, ah, coven meetings?" Dr. Prong pursued.

"To be scientifically illuminated, of course." Simeon smiled gently. "Don't worry: it doesn't hurt – much. We actually haven't lost a candidate since Judge Crater. Never could get that blighter back from the Pink Dimension."

"I think you're putting me on," Roger Prong said, losing his neutral tone.

Simeon laughed. "Good," he said cheerfully. "You have the right attitude. But don't carry it too far. Think how surprised you'll be if we push you through the Pink Dimension and you land in Fernando Poo – with King Kong as your companion, say."

Dr. Prong sat bolt upright. "You – " he gasped. "You're one of *them*."

Dill also sat upright, thinking that Simeon had pushed one of the wrong buttons on the dotty doctor. Before he could speak, however, Simeon's rich laugh rang out again.

"Not at all," he said calmly. "I just happen to know that you're very sensitive to those words right now, although I don't know what they mean to you. You were having a bad dream a while back and muttering very apprehensively, and those were the two names I caught. However, I have other tactics for getting into your subconscious, so be prepared for further shocks. It's all part of your illumination."

"What *is* illumination?" Stella asked.

"Seeing your own face exactly as it was before your father and mother conceived you," Simeon answered simply. He turned onto Sheridan Road.

"Oh," Stella said, "that reincarnation shit. I'm hip."

"Reincarnation is the furthest thing from what I mean," Simeon said quietly. He frowned thoughtfully and then began talking at some length, and – perhaps due to his somewhat florid speaking style, perhaps to the various alcoholic and other chemicals coursing through their blood streams – they could all visualize quite clearly what he told them.

It all began, he said, in Atlantis.

It was the festival of the great goddess Mum-Mum, the Mother of All Life. Lhuv-Kerapht and Klarkash-Ton, the high priests, watched with glinting and glittering eyes as the devout filed into the temple. Atlantis was a very old, very pious civilization and the citizens had prepared themselves for the most important religious event in the Atlantean five-season calendar, the Epiphany of Mum-Mum, at which the divine and mysterious *T'angpoon* (serpent) power was evoked and everybody in the temple, as the current slang expression had it, "went ape." The devout had smoked the magic herb, *Ak-opoko-gol,* and were in a happy and mellow state long before getting to the cathedral. Much was expected.

The priestess Salome lay upon the altar, tense and expectant, her young heart overflowing with mixed pride and humility to think that she had been selected for this all-important rite, on which the crops for the next year depended. For she knew, as all Atlantis did, that only if Mum-Mum were pleased and satisfied that this rite were correctly performed – "with joy and beauty," as the ancient *Pnakotic Manuscripts* said – would she bless the fields and bring forth abundant corn, rice and *ak-opoko-gol* next spring.

Salome was, like all those who had gathered there on that holiest of holy days, nude; for it was of ancient teaching in Atlantis that clothing, as a mark of rank and caste, should never enter the temple of the High Gods where all were equal. Besides, clothing got in the way when the worship service became really lively, as always happened during the festival of Mum-Mum.

Lhuv-Kerapht began the chant, "Come thou forth, IAO, come thou forth and shed thy light upon us."

"IAO, IAO, IAO," Klarkash-Ton chanted.

"IAO, IAO, IAO," the congregation repeated.

"Father and Mother are One God: *Ararita!*" Lhuv-Kerapht chanted.

"Mother and Son are One God: *Ararita!*" Klarkash-Ton chanted.

"Son and Daughter are One God: *Ararita!*" the congregation chanted.

"Father and Daughter are One God: *Ararita!*" Lhuv-Kerapht chanted.

"Glory to the Father and to the Mother and to the Son and to the Daughter," Klarkash-Ton chanted. "Glory to the internal Holy Spirit and glory to the external Holy Spirit. For here are not six nor five nor four nor three nor two nor one nor none. *Ararita! Ararita! Ararita!*"

"Partake of the sacrament," Salome chanted, spreading her legs. Lhuv-Kerapht knelt before the altar and kissed her forehead, saying, "In the name of the Father." He kissed her right breast, shouting, "In the name of the Son." He kissed her left breast, whispering, "In the name of the Daughter." He kissed her pussy, screaming, "In the name of the Mother."

Then he climbed upon her and began to partake of the sacrament.

("Wow, that's what I call a sacrament," Tarantella commented.

"It's the earliest and most powerful sacrament," Simeon Luna said gravely.)

As Lhuv-Kerapht had kissed the priestess's forehead, she had activated her pineal gland, which is located there, and began to *skry*, or perceive, in the Astral. As he kissed her breasts, she activated the heart chakra, and the spirit of Mum-Mum, Mother of all Life, possessed her. As he kissed her pussy, the *T'angpoon* energy (which later civilizations were to call *kundalini, mana,* Animal Magnetism or just "the vibes") became activated also and each person in the temple felt its faint, unmistakable *tingle* in the air. "Strong is the Serpent Power," Klarkash-Ton shouted, as he felt it.

"Strong is the Serpent Power," chanted the congregation.

Two hours later – for these rites take much longer than the
common or garden variety of sex known to the profane and
unilluminated – Lhuv-Kerapht was still slowly and patiently
partaking of the sacrament within Salome's ever-hotter pussy.
The entire congregation had grouped itself into pairs, or
occasionally in trios or quartets, and were also partaking. Only
Klarkash-Ton, sunk deep in meditation, remained uninvolved
in the physical part of the Great Work; for it was through his
mind that Mum-Mum, would eventually, communicate.

Upon the walls, the carvings of men and women in every
imaginable sexual combination looked down ecstatically upon
the similar ecstasy of the men and women of the congregation,
also intertwined in every imaginable sexual combination. And
still the Serpent Power increased; almost everybody, even the
least sensitive, could see the auras and psionic fields in the air
now.

One hour later, the congregation had "*gone ape*" as the
Atlantean slang expressed it. All were "speaking in tongues,"
the ancient primate language that antedates humanity; many
beat their chests, without stopping a moment in the slow,
rhythmic nonorgasmic sex pulsation. The *T'angpoon* possessed
them all, and cellular energies, molecular awarenesses, atomic
and genetic intelligences manifested among them: the true
gods, which appear to external vision as stars.

There was not a single person in the church aware of
the bodies and other so-called "tangible objects" which
compromise ordinary perception. Turned on to the subatomic
Direct Perception which is the intercommunication of the
universe itself, they saw and felt only the energetic level *which
is aware of its own immortality*. People had come to the temple,
but only gods were in attendance now.

And then Mum-Mum spoke, through Klarkash-Ton.
"Behold, I am infinite space and the infinite stars thereof. I
am Mum-Mum and my number is twenty-three and my word
is Abrahadabra. Bad news; Atlantis is sinking. The earth is

shifting its crust. No malice intended, anymore than you mean harm if you stretch your legs. Be of good cheer: death is the wildest joke of all."

"Blessed be Mum-Mum," Lhuv-Kerapht had presence of mind to recite. "*Earth abides!*" And he galloped, at last, the rites complete, into his orgasm, just a split second before the walls began to walk.

"Nonsense," Dr. Prong said promptly, as the others in the car looked at Reverend Luna with open mouths. "I don't believe in magic. It's all superstition and tommyrot. Besides, if they were all killed, who left a record of that day for you?"

"I was there," Simeon Luna said simply. "I was Lhuv-Kerapht. And you," he said to Stella, "were Salome."

CHAPTER FIFTEEN

Does a dog have Buddha?

Markoff Chaney slept, looking for all the world like the most innocent child in the most sentimental fantasy of Charles Dickens, except, of course, that like most males he slept with a slight hard-on – a physiological symptom, as doctors have recently discovered, that he was dreaming.

As the midget slept and dreamed, various stealthy figures came to his door, fished around in the lock with various instruments and slunk away, frustrated by the bolt he had installed. None of them intended to rob or harm him, however; they were of that brigade of Gay and prehensive oralists who haunt all YMCAs at night. Undisturbed, the little nihilist wandered on and on into the plastic universe of Will which we slightingly call unconsciousness.

Often, he smiled, with all the innocent charm of the child he so hauntingly resembled.

"Married!" Mary Kelly said rapturously. "Next Sunday! Oh, isn't it wonderful?"

"Yeah, wonderful," Stan said, somewhat less enthusiastically. He had visions of herds, flocks, *regiments* of kids, all looking like Mary's mother, all with jam and other icky and sticky things on their fingers, all pounding each other over the heads with various plastic toys while he tried to watch football on TV. "Yeah, wonderful," he repeated mechanically.

"And you're wonderful, too!" the darling girl cried abruptly, planting a big wet kiss on his mouth. Immediately, to his intense surprise, his prick stiffened a bit. She noticed. "My Lord," she said in awe, "You're ready *again*?" A light of Irish mischief sparkled in her eyes. "Well, I'll fix that." And her mouth descended, for the second time in her young life, to encompass a real he-man male sex organ; she shivered with delight.

"I don't think I'm ready *yet*," Stan started to say. Then, he felt the first wave rising. "I guess I am," he said happily. He was both surprised and delighted at this new side of Mary Kelly's personality.

"Here," he said, the soul of gallantry, "let me make it nice for you, too." And he gently shifted her about on the couch and dived head-first into her pussy.

"Oh," Mary said, taking her mouth from his penis. "That's nice. Where did you learn *that*?"

"It was in the *Pussycat Advisor* last month," he said "How to save a failing marriage, I think. It's called *Sox ant nerve*. That's French," he added, showing his sophistication.

"*Sox ant nerve,*" she repeated rapturously. "Let's do it some more!"

Stan gallantly obliged, finding her clitoris quickly and circling it with slow tongue movements. Hell, this wasn't as bad as some of the jokes said. It actually tasted – nice. And it was groovy to feel her mouth kissing and licking and sucking on his tool while he did this. Maybe the priests were always saying *Pussycat* was a dirty magazine, but it sure was educational.

"Mrs. Svenson, what's wrong with my marriage?" the TV asked in a desperate female voice. "Veil," another female voice answered, "maybe you should try swamp-grown coffee. Dat's the best kind."

Mary Kelly hardly heard. The tongue in her pussy seemed to reach up to the very center of her being; she hardly felt

 The Sex Magicians

like a body at all anymore, but like a balloon with the skin
off, all airy and floating free, with that tongue of flame at the
very center of her, radiating out in wave after wave like some
star almost; it reminded her, oddly, of some expression from
the church, what was it, oh, yes, the Gift of Tongues, what
a lovely expression. And meanwhile, she was finding to her
own amazement, a nice big cock in the mouth is a wonderful
experience. Almost like nursing at the breast again. How sweet,
she thought girlishly, to think of it that way. "Mum-Mum," she
breathed hoarsely, nursing happily, until suddenly the flame
exploded into wildfire and she rose and rose again and again,
spasming, expanding, hardly hearing herself shout in the midst
of her suckling, "Chrise mu cunt mu cunt Chrise . . ."

Stan was astonished; he had never known nice girls could
suck cock with such enthusiasm or push their hot little pussies
into your mouth with such reckless abandon. My God, he
thought rapturously, it's almost like having a movie actress or
the Pussycat of the Month. He almost came himself at the end
of her spasm.

"Chrise," he heard her mutter. "Oh my Lord. Oh Jesus." And
then in a zonked voice: *"Let's do it again!"*

He quickly dived back into her pussy, moving his tongue in
loops from the clit to the vaginal opening, back to the clit, back
to the vagina, determined to come again himself this time as
her enthusiastic mouth hotly gripped the head of his whang.

The doorbell rang.

"Oh piss, shit and corruption!" Mary cried. "My parents!"

"It can't be," Stan gasped. "They're in Lake Geneva." He
crept to the window and peeked out. "Oh," he breathed in
relief, "It's only your brother, Johnny. And some girl."

The doorbell ceased, and in its place came the faint but
unmistakable sound of a key in the lock.

"Jesus H. Particular Christ," Stan moaned, "what'll we *do?*"

But Mary smiled a strange smile. "What will be, will be,"

she said. "This night is some kind of turning point."

And the suddenly brazen girl abruptly knelt down by the couch, took his penis in her hand and began sucking it again.

"My God," Stan started to protest.

"We're caught red-handed anyway," she said, pausing. She returned to the job, sucking more vigorously.

Stan looked up, terrified, as young Johnny Kelly walked into the room, eyes opening in amazement as he took in the interesting scene. The girl with him – Stan faintly recognized her as the Portinari's daughter, Bea, the one who entered a convent but then dropped out – gasped audibly.

"Well," Johnny Kelly said finally, "my little sister is growing up."

Mary Kelly slowly turned around and faced him. Stan felt his penis start to shrivel at once; it was a tense situation no matter how you sliced it. He was scared.

"Remember when we were both fourteen?" Mary asked. "You wanted me to do this to you, and I refused. I'm sorry now. I didn't know how *good* it was." She spoke with great vehemence staring at Johnny hotly.

"Bravo," the Portinari girl said. "You're finally growing up, Mary."

"Yeah," Stan added helpfully. "Growing up." He laughed nervously.

Johnny Kelly stared at his sister, white around the lips. "It's never too late to make amends," he said, slightly flushed.

"Hey, wait a minute –" Stan protested.

"Don't be a spoilsport," the Portinari girl said to him. "It's *always* more fun with four."

Stan looked at her again, realizing what a classy dish she was. "Well," he said dubiously, but with a tone of hope.

"Good," Mary Kelly said. "That's decided. What will we do first?"

"And now," the TV announced suddenly, "our midnight sermonette with Reverend Father Francis X. Treponema."

"This is my first night," Mary Kelly said boldly, "I want you *all* to do me."

"Oh, wow," Miss Portinari said. "Just like that time in the convent when I had three sisters doing me at once. But you'll have two men, plus me. Oh, wow. Far out!"

Father Treponema's bland face stared warmly out of the TV screen, looking down upon a moving spectacle. "Let us pray," he said, "Oh, God, our Father in heaven, give us strength to carry out every project we undertake and not to be shirkers. Give us strength to carry through to the finish and never to be quitters. Lead us in thy ways, Oh Lord . . ."

The position agreed upon had Mary lying on her side between her brother and Stan. As Stan gamily, a bit nervously still, plugged away at her hot littlypussy, Johnny began navigating the more difficult pass between her buttocks, gradually worming his way an inch, two inches, three inches, as passion released her muscular armoring. The lovely Beatrice Portinari, meanwhile, was busily engaged in kissing Mary all over the face, shoulders, neck, breasts, muttering little endearments – things like, "Nice hot prick in ums cunt, baby, Nice hot prick. And brother's prick in ums ittle assy-wassy, ha, babes? Two nice pricks," and so on, with more and more, hotter and hotter kisses.

"Give me your *twat*," Mary screamed finally. "Yes, brethren and sistren," Father Treponema was continuing, "success in life is not for the lazy or the indifferent. Success is for the hard workers, the men of vision and guts –"

Beatrice shifted around and presented her pussy to Mary's tongue. Immediately, it entered her and she leaned forward eagerly to kiss Johnny on the lips. "Oh, bugger her good," she moaned. "Set her ass on fire. Make her happy, she's sucking my pussy so nicely."

Mary, meanwhile, feeling the two pulsating-hot cocks

plowing away inside her and driving her higher and higher in dizzy waves of pleasure, concentrated on the taste of pussy, which she had never known before. She licked raptly, all over the inside, clit and vage and all, and around the lips and into the bush and over the thighs and back to the vage again, loving every part of it, almost out of her mind with the double sensation of two cocks and the flavor of cunt. "Only the weak look to government aid," a voice was droning somewhere, "but those who have Jesus in their hearts can find their own happiness." Mary pursued her own happiness, bouncing happily between the two cocks like a puppy being petted, licking and sucking on a cunt for the first time in her life, totally zonked.

Stan had found that he could play with both of the Portinari girl's titties while fucking Mary's cunt, and this was a most interesting sensation indeed. By stretching a little, he was even able to suck on one of her nipples, which immediately grew hard in his mouth. She looked at him, smiling blissfully, and he realized she was about to come from the delights of Mary's eager little tongue up inside her cunt. He sucked harder on the nipple, feeling her beginning spasms; this keyed him off in turn and he felt his cock spurting into Mary's hot pussy. Mary started to come then, feeling each separate spurt of the cock inside her and actually tasting the change in Beatrice's cunt flow as Beatrice came. Johnny went wild, fucking her ass almost hard enough to hurt; this catapulted her into a second orgasm immediately, and she felt Johnny coming inside her too, crying out loud "Oh, Jesus, my *brother's* come up inside my *ass*. Oh, Jesus!"

All four lay silent and exhausted, barely breathing.

"And God be with you always," Father Treponema concluded as the organ music rose.

Back at Sput's mansion, things were, by comparison, calming down. Most of the guests had left, in fact. Sput sat on a

                    The Sex Magicians

floor pillow, toking occasionally at his hookah and lecturing to the only audience left, the butler and two Pussiettes.

The butler listened politely; he was aware that the Great Man needed to have somebody listen to his metaphysical and cosmic speculations. The two Pussiettes, long since stoned out of their skulls into the middle of next Thursday, were lying on the rug languidly and limpidly sixty-nineing; in fact, they had been doing that for nearly an hour now.

Sput watched the two girls philosophically. Neither had had an orgasm for nearly thirty minutes, although both had climaxed several times earlier in their play. "Why do they continue?" he asked rhetorically. "They don't *need* another orgasm, and they're not consciously aiming for one, I'll wager. They are lost in the process itself, like Taoists or alchemists. This is practical experimental mysticism we're watching, Jameson."

"Yes, sir," Jameson said. "You express it very well, sir."

"And they're not dykes, not really," Sput went on. "I know. I've had each of them on numerous occasions. Good in the hay, too. *Both* of them." He toked again, thinking deeply. "And yet here they are, cozy as Gertrude Stein and Alice B. Toklas. Why? Because they got coupled up like that in the heat of the orgy, and they haven't found any good reason to stop. And why is that? Has the goddamn hashish fucked up their minds? I don't think so. I think it's straightened out their minds. There *is* no reason to stop. Sex *is* good, all sex, hetero or homo or in any permutations. It's the best thing in the world. Anybody who says different is a damned motherfucking liar or a neurotic. Right?"

"Right, sir." The butler suppressed a yawn.

Sput watched the Pussiettes licking raptly at each other's hairy cunts, eyes closed in bliss. "Of such is the kingdom of Heaven," he concluded thoughtfully.

The butler yawned again.

Sput heaved himself to his feet. "The whole world is crazy," he said. "Literally crazy. Stark raving mad. Imagine, there are guys busy tonight, crawling through stinking fly-infested jungles to blow up other guys – or women and children even. And other guys trying to square the circle or find subatomic particles smaller than the quark. Imagine! when we could all be balling each other. The whole world is mad." He lumbered over to the girls. "*Chickies*," he said cooingly, "*the rooster is crowing.*"

"Very good, sir," the butler said, between his teeth. "May I leave now, sir?"

"Umm, yes," Sput mumbled. He was flat on his back now, and maneuvering the two girls into a position he had just remembered from a Tijuana specialty act. Briefly, he had one of the girls sitting upon his waist, taking his penis in her snatch, and was maneuvering the other upon his shoulders so she could have his tongue in her own moist little pussy. "Now," he said, "kiss and play with each other's titties and go on with the dyke action. *You're* Gloria Steinem and *you're* Kate Millet, got it?"

"Good evening, sir," the butler said, withdrawing.

"Mum-Mum," Sput gasped, buried in pussy.

The butler headed straight for the kitchen. When the cook saw him coming, she knew what to expect immediately. Putting down her newspaper, she reached in the drawer and took out a vibrator.

And still Markoff Chaney slept the sleep of the just, and still the stealthy figures crept to his door, grappled with the bolt, muttered "Crap," and crept away again.

CHAPTER SIXTEEN

Who is the third who walks always beside you?

"A Mama Vibe," Simeon Luna was explaining as they sat about his kitchen munching caviar and crackers, "is a Vibe that unites with all other Vibes, like an active radical in chemistry. Dig?"

"I don't believe in Vibes," Dr. Prong said promptly. Everybody ignored him.

"You mean," Josh Dill said gropingly, "it's a kind of ESP that broadcasts on all channels at once?"

"Ez-actly!" Simeon beamed. "No matter where your attention is, no matter what mental channel your internal TV is set on, a Mama Vibe comes right in and replaces the normal 'show' on that wave length. And on everybody else's internal TV screen, too. In short, it becomes the 'reality' that everybody is experiencing at that moment. Mass telepathic hypnosis."

"I don't believe in telepathy," Dr. Prong said.

"Far fucking out," Stella said thoughtfully. "And somebody in Chicago is broadcasting a Mama Vibe?"

"A *very horny* Mama Vibe," Reverend Luna said. "Haven't you all been more sexually active than usual?"

"*I'll say,*" Tarantella commented with a delicious grin.

"Well," Simeon Luna said, "that's because you're all acting out the unconscious and preconscious fantasies of the individual who's sending out this Mama Vibe. In a sense, you're all living in his head, or *her* head, whoever this person is. You're like characters in a book, and you've got to do what the author imagines you doing."

"Thank God he's not on a sadomaso kick," Josh Dill said with a nervous grin.

"That, however, is a distinct possibility for the next stage of this process," Simeon said bluntly. "More and more unconscious material is coming up in these projected fantasies, and everybody has a nasty spot somewhere in his Id. When our broadcaster gets that deep into his or her psyche, all hell will break loose. That's why we've got to find him or her and deactivate this Vibe."

'This is getting *heavy*," Stella said.

"I still don't believe a word of it," Dr. Prong said primly, crossing his arms.

"How many people are – uh – receiving this broadcast?" Dill asked.

"Everyone within fifty miles of the broadcaster is getting a strong dose of it," Simeon said. "It gets weaker and weaker beyond that point."

"And how did the broadcaster acquire this power to send out Mama Vibes?" Josh asked.

"By accident, I'm sure." Simeon frowned thoughtfully. "Anybody who knew what he was doing would be more careful and selective. This person just stumbled on it. There are many techniques to focus the mind – Tibetan *mandalas*, the hexagrams from the Chinese *I Ching* or *Book of Changes*, the *Tarot* fortune-telling cards. If the culprit was concentrating on any of them while he was in a horny mood, he'd start broadcasting a Mama Vibe without being aware of it."

"Now wait a fucking minute," Stella said. "I use the *I Ching* for divination all the time. Do you mean to say I'm broadcasting Mama Vibes every time I do that?"

"Oh, not at all," Simeon said laughing. "If it were that easy, there'd be no so-called reality at all, just a million and one conflicting test-patterns. A man could walk through his kitchen door and find himself in Perth Amboy or Benares; or you could pick up a pencil to write with and find a cobra in your hand. Thank Goddess that magic – broadcasting Mama Vibes – isn't *that* easy. No: what is needed is very special circumstances. First, the proper shapes to draw the brain to a focus – Tarot or Ching or mandala shapes. But after, the *T'angpoon* or *kundalini* energy has to be activated in the spine, and the pineal gland, or Third Eye, in the forehead, and the person has to be in a state of maximum sexual excitation for quite a long time: less than an hour will seldom do. Finally, there has to be a strong emotional frustration, a sense that there's something wrong with reality as it presently is, something that has to be fixed. Find a person with all those things going at once, and you've got a Mama Vibe being broadcast."

"And if you can't stop this Mama Vibe?" Josh Dill asked carefully.

"Reality will never be the same in old Chicago," Simeon said simply.

Our heroine, the darling Josie Welch, meanwhile, was still afloat in a universe of Fuck.

Marvin Gardens had set up a chess problem and was staring at the board in deep concentration, only bothering to make a note on his M.O.Q. sheet when she reached another climax. He was no longer completely unaffected, however: he intended to visit the men's room in Lincoln Park as soon as his shift here ended. Marvin was a devotee of what his set called Tea Room Trade.

Josie knew and cared nothing about this. She and her lover/ co-pilot, the ninety billion year old ACE computer (who still had a voice somewhat like HAL-9000 in 2001) were zooming deeper and deeper into the Ovum Galaxy in the center of the marvelous universe of Fuck. "This is the center of space time," ACE was purring in that soft, tigerish voice of his, "and it is also the center of your womb, darling Josie. It is way, way out and it is also way, way in. You can only enter this mystery of mysteries on vibes of sheer ecstasy, because all matter at lower vibratory rates gets destroyed by the antimatter fields at the perimeter of this galaxy. So, in order to navigate this dangerous crossing, I must fuck you even more deeply, my darling,"

"Oh, do it, ACE, do it to me good," she murmured, "I want to see the center of the universe."

"There, there," he purred, "you'll see the center of the universe when your pretty little cunt gets hot enough again."

"Take me," she moaned, "take me to the center of space time." And deep, deep into her cunt and deep, deep into the energy mesh of raw creation ACE piloted her. Slow permutations, like the growth of crystals, her sensations were scarcely contaminated by thought or vision: deep, deep they went, down into a cavern of strange floral energies, each petal shape tingling with the languid tingles in the petals of her own moist pussy, the shaft of the actual ACE machine digging deeper and deeper into her vaginal barrel, her womb moving slightly with each thrust, one vast star-sponge permeating all space time with the same vibe. "Oh, ACE, oh, ACE, you fuck so divinely," she gasped.

"It's the only way to travel," he purred.

"Oh, keep fucking me. Keep fucking me. Please, please, keep fucking me."

Down, down into the center of the star sponge they plunged.

And still the Mama Vibe pulsated through space time.

Hugo de Naranja had been a milkman in the Garfield Park section of Chicago for twenty-three years and had seen some strange sights in the early morning hours. This particular morning, however, was turning into a ring-a-ding that he'd never forget.

The first shock had occurred while he was making his

delivery to the Convent of Saint Theophobia. As always, he opened the back gate and placed the six-pack of milk on the walk leading toward the kitchen door. But then, as he was about to tiptoe back out again, moving lights and strange noises in the garden caught his attention. Curious, he took a few steps forward. And there, under the trees, he saw a strange procession.

Mother Claustrophilia, the abbess, was leading the nuns, each bearing a candle, in some kind of dance or orgy. They were all stark naked, shocking enough in itself, but the chant was hardly in Church Latin. It was plain ordinary English, and poor Hugo's ears burned when he recognized the melody.

It was "Mister Wong Has the Biggest Tong in Chinatown."

Hugo quickly hurried back to his truck, not sure whether to believe his eyes and ears.

A few stops later, he came upon an equally startling spectacle.

It was the Cackler residence, home of the worst grouch in Hugo's whole route, Harold Cackler, president of NOODLE (National Organization Organized for Decent Literature and Entertainment.) Cackler was a man forever complaining that his milk was sour or that he had ordered cream and gotten buttermilk or one damn thing or another; besides that, he was a perpetual crusader for greater and greater power to the police in order to enable them to supervise every waking moment of every citizen. SUPPORT YOUR LOCAL WIRE TAPPER: CLEAN-MINDED PEOPLE HAVE NO SECRETS said a large bumper sticker on his car.

Hugo privately considered Mr. Cackler a nut. And, now, on this amazing morning, just as the first rays of dawn began to appear in the sky, as Hugo eased open the porch door of the Cackler house to place two quarts of milk in the vestibule, a hoarse and passionate voice bellowed, "Now, Shirley, now!"

Startled, Hugo almost dropped his bottles.

"Bathe me in your golden showers!" the voice ranted on.

"Piss all over me, my darling!"

Hugo set the bottles down gently, as if trying to avoid detection by the most delicate seismograph in the world. Mr. Cackler, he realized, would not appreciate being observed in whatever sort of act he was accomplishing.

"Oh, darling, darling," the voice gibbered insanely.

Hugo could no longer resist. With all the delicacy of Nijinsky, he went up on his toes and took only two dainty steps to reach the window to the living room area. There an astonishing sight greeted his eyes.

Mr. Cackler, his face blackened by burnt cork, was lying on the floor. Above him, held most tenderly, was one of those cutie-pie "life-size" dolls that, as the ads say, *wets itself*. "Do it again, Shirley darling," Cackler howled, holding a bottle to the doll's rosy lips, "Pee all over yo' old Bojangles!" The doll immediately discharged from the bottom the water entering at the top. "Darling, darling," Cackler moaned. The maniac obviously thought he was Bill "Bojangles" Robinson, the great Negro tap dancer of the 1930s, and that the doll was Shirley Temple.

It takes all kinds, Hugo thought philosophically, as he tiptoed away.

This was turning into one bizarre morning.

Half an hour later came the most unforgettable stop of all, at the usually sedate Kelly residence.

Scarcely had Hugo deposited two bottles in the box next to the front door when the door itself burst open and young Mary, who was always so prim, stood there, in her birthday suit.

"Mother of God," Hugo breathed piously. This was indeed a Morning To Remember.

"Are you a Nigra?" the girl asked tensely.

"No, I am a Puerto Rican," Hugo said with dignity, pronouncing it as they did back on the Island: *poo-air-to reecan.*

"Well, I wanted a nigger, but you'll do."

A gigantic Pollack appeared behind her, also naked as a jaybird. He held ten dollars in his hand. "Do we interest you?" he asked.

"You bet!" Hugo cried excitedly. I am going to fuck a White Protestant Girl, he thought ecstatically, although on one level he knew very well that the Irish were Catholics, too. It didn't matter. All white girls were by definition Protestant.

Inside, two other young people, naked as angels, were sitting on the floor looking at him with interest as he entered.

Two white Protestant girls, Hugo thought, almost flipping.

"We need a fifth," Mary Kelly explained briefly.

"We've been trying to manage with four and it just doesn't work."

"At your service, ma'am," Hugo said gallantly, quietly pocketing the ten dollars at the same time. The other girl, a dark one, was probably Italian; her pussy, while lush and pleasant enough, might have been found home on the Island. He had eyes for the Kelly girl, whose pussy had a reddish fur that was more Caucasian and Protestant in his mind. Mother Mary, he thought piously, may I get a chance to suck on that Irish pussy for a while.

He could imagine the scene in the pool hall when he told about it later. The guys would be bragging about how far into the dangerous area of White Pussy they had pushed – "I had an Italian girl once," "Yeah, well I had a pure-blooded French girl," that kind of crap – and he would announce, casually, "I had an Irish girl, *with red hair*, and she let me suck her pussy!!!" Boy, would their eyes bug out.

Except that they'd never believe him.

Well, fuck that. He would know in his heart that it was true.

"What do I do?" he asked.

The position was quickly explained and Hugo breathed

another prayer to the Holy Mother. It was even better than he had hoped for. And I, he thought, am virtually the cornerstone.

(Anyone attached to white Protestant pussy, in his mind, was the cornerstone.)

Mary Kelly, twenty three years old and rapidly becoming an adult, sat in a rocking chair as the Puerto Rican sat on the floor and began to lap gently at her thighs. He rapidly turned black in her mind, and she waited anxiously for his tongue to enter her cunt. Johnny carefully climbed onto the arms of the rocker and grabbed hold of the curtain rod over the doorway to the kitchen. Mary leaned forward and mouthed on his penis raptly, imagining that he was Father Ryan from the local church. "Normally," Father Ryan said in her fantasy, "I would consider it Sin for you to let that black buck lick your hot little pussy that way, Mary, but since you're giving me such a classy blow job, I guess I'll be tolerant this time. *Pax vobiscum*, kid." And he gravely blessed her, taking away all sin and guilt, while she relaxed into the pulsing pleasure of the moist Sidney Poitier tongue up deep inside her wet steamy cunt.

Johnny, balancing on the arms of the rocking chair and holding onto the curtain rod, rocked slowly at first, noting with delight that Mary was more and more relaxed and taking his cock deeper and deeper into her mouth and throat. He fucked rhythmically into the girl's mouth, hearing the chair creak as they coupled together. Fucking a mouth, he thought blissfully, is in some ways even better than fucking a cunt. The tongue moved around his hard hot cock and sent little shivers up his body as he fucked deep, deep into her throat, watching her eyes close in a delirium of pleasure. It was even better, he reflected, because she was his sister and he had longed for this kind of super sex with her so many times in his early adolescent fantasies.

Stan, watching his beloved Mary suck on her brother's big cock while the milkman lapped around inside her pussy, felt a jealousy strangely mixed with pride and pleasure. One thing was sure: Mary certainly wasn't the prissy little prude she had been only a few hours ago. As Beatrice Portinari sprawled on the floor and began licking Hugo's ass, Stan knelt behind and began buggering her hot pretty little ass, watching avidly as Johnny's cock moved rhythmically in and out of Mary's mouth. He imagined he was going into Beatrice's mouth for a second then came back to the tight hot sensation of her ass, hearing her moan slightly.

Gee, Protestants can be nice people, too, Hugo was thinking as the Italian girl licked his ass. He slurped around in the Irish pussy, feeling like a Knight who has finally found the Holy Grail. White Protestant Pussy, he thought, White Protestant Pussy: I love it. He munched on the clitoris passionately, wishing they would believe him when he told about this at the pool hall.

Johnny slowly raised his feet from the arms of the rocking chair, hanging suspended by his grip on the curtain rod. Every muscle in his body was under maximum tension and the energy spasms starting in his whang immediately multiplied. This is the purpose of the position he was using, which is called a Flying Philadelphia Fuck, even though it was not invented in Philadelphia but in the wide-open nearby town of Camden, New Jersey, where the folk are so devoted to extreme and excruciating pleasures as to have made even exciting metropolitan Philadelphia seem staid by comparison. As Johnny hung there, Mary rocked rapidly back and forth, taking her brother's strained and monstrously enlarged cock deeper and deeper into her throat, feeling him begin to spasm and ejaculate hot white spurts deep down inside her, almost burning with intensity. She immediately was galvanized into a climax of her own, thrusting her cunt madly upward into the air, rubbing all around the milkman's mouth and nose, feeling his black tongue far up inside the tunnel of her spasmodic vagina, almost tickling her womb.

Hugo, maddened by the Irish pussy coming in his mouth, spurted again and again on the carpet, heaving like a wrestler, driving Beatrice into a new excess of passion as he pushed her tongue deeper into his ass. White Protestant girls, he thought in absolute para-Nirvana, white Protestant girls!

Beatrice Portinari, aflame with fires of insane joy, lapped at the milkman's ass, feeling Stan's cock harder and deeper inside her own spasmodic rectum. Bugger, bugger, she thought divinely, thrusting upward to take the stiff prick deeper inside her butt, beginning to explode into total superorgasm in ass and pussy at once.

And then the curtain rod broke.

Falling, tumbling, over and over in air, all five felt as if they were in free fall, null-gravity, spinning toward the center of space, in blissful total mouth-ass-cock-pussy fuck, unending, world without time.

CHAPTER SEVENTEEN

What is outside Space?

"Believe me," Simeon Luna said, "This is the only way to track down a Mama Vibe."

The others, sitting nude on the floor of the temple in the midst of a sunburst design upon a thick Persian rug, nodded thoughtfully. Josh had no particular religion and had long ago concluded that the Reverend Luna's Scientific Illuminism, whatever the deuce it was, made some kind of sense. Tarantella and Stella, both long-time devotees of *I Ching* and Occultism in general, were aware that Simeon was a studly old dude who probably knew something or other about Vibes of all sorts. Dr. Prong, passionately wed to the religion of Pure Science, still objected; but the foul drug they had given him had created such a rosy glow that he decided to keep his doubts to himself and have a good time.

"Basically, what you'll be doing is a kind of remembering," Simeon went on. "Most of life is forgetting. Concentrating on one thing at a time, in a linear fashion, like the words on a page. Illumination is remembering the whole context, all at once. It's all in your own minds, of course, and I'm merely drawing it forth. We need five minds together – that's the *funfwissenschaft*, or science of fives, which our founder, Adam Weishaupt, found during a game of strip poker in old Ingolstadt two centuries ago."

Simeon seemed about to add something on that topic, but then thought better off it.

"Well," he said, "shall we begin? Stella, Dr. Prong?"

Feeling like a fool but still enjoying himself, Roger Prong turned and put his arms about Stella.

"Just hug each other and look into each other's eyes," Simeon said. "Just hold it like that. Think, now. Don't speak, either of you. Dr. Prong, when you *know* she's ready, begin to mount her. Don't look anywhere but her eyes. You don't know who she is. You don't know who you are. What is there that you do know? Look into her eyes and find it, the one thing that you do know beyond all doubt or argument. Think now, as you look into her eyes."

Roger felt more like a fool, but enjoyed it more. The eyes confronting him, feminine and strangely wise, seemed to know without once looking downward just how fast he was becoming hard. Suddenly the eyes *knew* that he knew and they were calling him, in a language beyond all the ambiguities of words. Roger moved forward, without a hesitation, and slipped his cock into her pussy; as he knew in advance, it was already warm, moist and ready for him.

"Now, Josh and Tarantella?" Simeon's voice was saying, from far away. Roger Prong was not quite hearing it. Stella's eyes were communicating with him; they were the eyes of her cunt, they told him what her cunt experienced. He floated through cunt, aware only of what cunt was telling him. He didn't even notice when Josh and Tarantella began fucking alongside him.

"Now," Simeon Luna intoned, "you will start to remember. Try to remember. In the universe of mind, what is believed to be true is true or becomes true, within limits to be learned only by experience. These limits are all to be transcended by further and deeper experience. In the universe of mind, there are no limits. Try to remember."

Roger slid moistly in cunt, his whole body bathed in electric pleasure, visual space disintegrating into the dimensionless space of pure sensation. This is what McLuhan means by tactile awareness, he thought with absorption.

     The Sex Magicians

"Don't hurry, don't hurry," Simeon chanted. "Float. Try to remember. What is remembered is believed true. What is believed true is true or becomes true. Try to remember."

Roger felt himself shifting his weight so he could use one hand to caress Stella's breasts and belly. He hadn't thought of doing that: he just found it happening. "Trust the wisdom of your body," Simeon said softly. "It knows what it wants. In your sleep each night, you adjust the covers without waking. This is the True Mind acting. Try to remember the True Mind. Try to remember the True Will. Usually, you only contact it in fantasy, in movies, in music, in pornography. Why do you not confront it directly? What do you fear? Try to remember."

Tarantella's body was like silk, like warm silk. But no – this was Stella's body. Or was it? Was he Roger Prong or was he Josh Dill? Did it matter? All that mattered was the universe of fuck and the slow spiral turn of her hips below him, the hungry mouth of her pussy devouring space and time, bringing him to the center of sensation.

"Slow, slow," Simeon crooned. "It can be much slower than you ever realized. It can take all of eternity. Try to remember. Everything happens in eternity. We only imagine that it is happening in time. Do you understand? Try to remember . . ."

Roger Prong, physician and scientist, began to realize that this crazy business, hypnotism or whatever it was, definitely centered him in the pleasure of sex as it occurred, instead of in the ego that was trying to control the pleasure and pace it. Beyond a certain point, he reflected, self-awareness obliterates itself, and beyond that point self-control becomes spontaneity. That was certainly a strange thought, but it seemed to be true. And meanwhile – due to those terrible drugs, no doubt – his consciousness was localized in his penis much more than was normal in his previous sex life. It was as if the penis thought instead of waiting for the head to think.

"What is experienced is believed," Simeon went on. "What is remembered is believed. Try to remember. You were, and are, a star, a god of one section of the universe. Remember? You split into nine parts, nine planets. Do try to remember. This is what it always was like and always will be like, this pleasure, this cosmic hummmmm. Each time you split it is the same. You never die, you only transform yourself. All nine of you split further, into millions of life forms, each of them strange and beautiful, or strange and frightening, to all the others. Try to remember. All of us, all of you, millions and millions of rays from the same Sun, the same Star of Heaven, all feeling the same *hummmmm* . . ."

The note continued, the cosmic, AUM, and Roger floated with it, alive with the tingle of Stella's cunt, the tingle that was merely the vibration of *mmmmmm*, through slow crystals of molecular awareness, patterns forming and reforming, a single dance.

"Look at your partner. Look, and see for yourself. See the one star that is us. Try to remember the one star that is us . . ."

Roger Prong, looking deep into Stella's eyes, saw his own reflection – but that's only a trick of optics, he reminded himself with scientific objectivity. But the emotion in those eyes, and his ability to read that emotion – who is communicating what to whom? The damned drug had fucked up his head. He couldn't remember what he was trying to do, he was just doing, going, being.

"What is the shape of your awareness, your experience? How old is it? How big is it? What color is it? Is it not one star, the one star it has always been? Are you not awakening finally from the nightmare of a completely imaginary cage around you? There is nothing around you, nothing restricting you, no limits to you, no limits anywhere. What you are experiencing is true. What you are experiencing is the real shape and size of you, and now you are remembering. Your true face before you were born. You are remembering. Your true face. Before. You were. Born . . ."

Roger Prong entered the White Light of the Void, and was

free for the first time in his life. Eternities later he saw Stella below him again and in her eyes he read that she was coming back also from the same journey to the center of the sun – that she, like himself, was being reborn into a body, a time, a place, but knew not who and what she really was, who and what he really was. With heart-stopping tenderness he kissed her lips and fucked very gently with her, feeling like Adam and Eve on the morning of creation, realizing how comical and how glorious it was to be human beings, male and female, while still being unborn, uncreated, unconditioned, unlimited.

There's *something* in this Scientific Illuminism, he thought.

"G. Rover Christ," the Reverend Luna said suddenly, "by all the pot-bellied gods of Bengal, it's a girl who's fucking with a machine!"

Dr. Prong blanched. "Josie," he said hoarsely.

And at that precise moment he felt himself explode inside Stella's warm and motherly cunt, a star-spurt of lions and dragons hurling toward her womb, crying involuntarily as all do at that moment, "IAO!"

CHAPTER EIGHTEEN

Who am I?

(Being a letter from Simeon Luna, D. D., to Roger Prong, Ph.D., M.D., LL.D., mailed from an undisclosed location somewhere in California):

Dear Dr. Prong:

I'm sure the events of that frantic morning left a marked impression upon you, and that you have often tried to interpret them – or correct them – to fit in with your notions of the "true" nature of "true" reality.

You saw how the Serpent Power – the kundalini or animal magnetism or orgone or psionic force or whatever one chooses to call it – was excited by the mild hypnotic suggestion I used while you and Stella copulated. You observed how I telepathically traced the Mama Vibe to a midget in a YMCA and a female experimental subject in your own laboratory. You came along in my Jaguar as we raced with the diminutive gentleman whose Tarot cards (of most original design) had served as the amplifier for the Mama Vibe broadcast. You also saw me speak privately at your laboratory with Experimental Subject Three A (Ms. J. W.)

In the next day's newspaper you noted the stories which confirmed that something odd had indeed been happening in Chicago in the past twenty-four hours. You read of the Kelly family, in which a respectable young brother and sister, together with two friends and a Puerto Rican milkman, were

arrested for aggravated exhibitionism, while staging a
Mongolian Cluster Fuck on their front lawn. You read
of how Joe Smith's wife, returning suddenly from
Wisconsin, found him and her own sister in a most
uncompromising position. You read dozens of similar
stories, including the especially sad and memorable
events involving the Mayor and the white female pig
in the stockyards. You found ample evidence to show,
in short, that a Mama Vibe had actually existed and
had provoked some rather extreme forms of sexual
behavior throughout the city of Chicago.

You probably deduced – correctly – that the small
gentleman at the YMCA and the randy lady known
as Experimental Subject Three A (dear Josie!) were
recruited by me, are now full-fledged members of the
Illuminati, and are being trained to use their powers
consciously and intelligently, without endangering
the delicate fabric of reality by premature outbursts of
senseless Magic.

Nevertheless, as a scientist, you must find all this hard
to believe.

I am sure that you have returned to the headquarters
of the Women's Christian Temperance Union in
Evanston, looking in vain for the sub-basement where
we of the Illuminati have our domain. You must have
been disappointed to discover that there is no such
sub-basement. Of course, I did not tell you our true
destination that night and in the dark you had no way
of knowing where I really took you.

We of the Illuminati do our jobs and then leave the
system, as a good medicine should. We do not linger
and take root, like a cancer. Most times, we do not
even reveal ourselves, and nobody knows we were
there – except the It Never Happened Department, but
under the oath which obliges me, I may not discuss
them.

Let it stand at that. I have departed for the somewhat

warmer climate from which I originally came. You
might not like it here – it *is*, hot and noisy, I'll admit –
but it's my home and I love it. Do not attempt to find
me. If it is our karma to meet again, *I* will find you.

In the universe of the mind, what is believed true
actually is true or becomes true, unless new beliefs
are formed.

Do what thou wilt shall be the whole of the law.

With very best regards,
Simeon Luna, Doctor of Divinity

(Being a letter from Josh Dill, Senior Editor, Tomcat
magazine, to Dr. Roger Prong):

. . . Ezra Pound is dead, in Italy, at the age of
eighty-seven. I don't really think he was the one who
was bothering you; more likely, it was some prankster
pretending to be Ezra Pound.

Yes, several Arabian mystic groups have had names
like Illuminati or Brothers of Light or Illuminated
Ones, etc. One of them, the Assassins of medieval
legend, are said to have introduced marijuana to the
Western world. The last widely publicized Illuminati
groups were headed by Adam Weishaupt in Bavaria,
circa 1770-1800, St. Martin in Paris during the same
years, and Aleister Crowley (who used the term
"Scientific Illuminism) in London circa 1900-1940.
Our intrepid research department says that various
conservative groups claim that the Illuminati still
exist and have taken over control of the whole world,
but this is not believed by sober and responsible
historians.

I'm convinced that Simeon Luna was putting us
on part of the time, but I'm not sure which part.
Sincerely,

Josh

Dr. Prong contemplated both letters over breakfast on a certain morning not long after these events. He thought about them further as he sipped his coffee and smoked his first cigarette of the day. Then he asked Stella, "What do you think sex is?" Stella, splendid and voluptuous in a black nightgown, said briefly, "Fun."

"No, seriously," the doctor said. "Is it chemicals that we feel in our bloodstream, or electricity between our cells, or some kind of magnetism, or what?"

"You think too much. It's just fun." Stella smiled softly, adding, "and it's about time to prepare for your day's work."

"No, just a minute. That *serpent power*, as Simeon Luna called it, still isn't recognized by orthodox science, and yet we all feel it every time we get sexually aroused . . ." Dr. Prong frowned thoughtfully. "I wonder what would happen if I took EEG.'s – brain waves, that is – on couples during intercourse and on trained yogis during their transcendental states. Hmmm? Would the waves be the same, maybe?"

"Well," Stella said, "that gives you another project to work on. Meanwhile, there's only a half hour before you have to leave for the laboratory, so if you're going to be prepared . . ."

"Yes," he said. "No more bad days like I've had in the past, thank goddess."

They tiptoed to the bedroom, his arm about her waist. "You are a love," he said gently, kissing her nose.

They approached the bed still on tiptoes and climbed in from opposite sides. Very gently, they leaned over Tarantella's still-sleeping body and began kissing her breasts, Roger working on the right titty and Stella on the left. The nude and magnificent Tarantella smiled softly in her sleep, like a great lioness, and then opened her eyes dreamily. "Morning?" she said.

Stella closed her mouth with a kiss. "Morning, dear," she said, inching a hand into Tarantella's crotch.

"Oh, you darlings," Tarantella said softly, as Roger covered her breasts and neck with kisses.

"You're the darling one," Roger said gallantly, working his finger into Tarantella's ass. "Comfy?" he asked.

"Exquisite," she said; and he began massaging her rectum gently, while Stella went on playing with her magnificent pussy. In a few moments, each of them was kissing and sucking one of Tarantella's nipples. While they worked this way, the big girl gasped, "Oh, cock. Give me a cock, in my mouth." Roger obediently hitched around and inserted his whang between Tarantella's ruby lips, where she immediately began sucking on it ravenously. By stretching, he kept the finger in her ass, massaging gently, while Stella petted and rubbed and tickled the whole cunt area. "Um, um," Tarantella gasped once, and then, between the hand in her ass and the hand in her snatch, she came to orgasm very slowly and raptly, with hardly any noise.

"That was *sweet*," she said happily, rolling over and beginning to suck on Stella's pussy. Dr. Prong shifted himself again and inserted his penis into Stella's mouth. "You sweet girls," he said happily. "You sweet, wonderful girls." Like a miser playing with his gold, he began running his hands over their four choice titties, squeezing gently, playing, rubbing, all the while smiling like the happiest Smiling Buddha in all China.

Stella's mouth got all hot around his prick and he realized she was coming. Tarantella, feeling the same heat in Stella's cunt, licked more passionately and Stella came with a great rising and falling like the ocean under a savage moon. "Yummy," she said.

Quickly, she took the doctor's cock back into her mouth and started sucking on it again. Tarantella switched around and, squeezing in like a puppy, began licking his balls.

"Oh, that's nice," Dr. Prong said. "That is so *goddamn* nice. Oh, don't stop. Oh, please don't stop. That is so lovely."

Tarantella quickly took both balls in her mouth and sucked very gently on them, while Stella pulled hard on his cock, sucking it way down into her throat. He put a hand on each of their heads, thrilled by their masses of glorious hair, and said again, "You darling girls, you. Oh, you darlings."

But then in a moment he cried weakly, "Stop now. Oh, stop."

The girls disengaged and lay back, two high-breasted and tremendous females, pussy hairs all wet and glistening beside him, smiling with utter contentment.

Roger mounted Tarantella first, fucking very slowly, stopping to plant little kisses on her mouth and Stella's mouth occasionally. When it was almost unbearable, he shifted and mounted Stella, sliding in easily, feeling the unique difference in the wiry quality of her pussy hair as compared to the silky softness of Tarantella's, but enjoying the similar warmth inside both cunts. "Oh, you darling girls," he said one more time, and then began fucking rapidly, pushing his penis hard and swift into the electro-magnetic pulsations of good fuck and true happiness that was the essence of cunt. When Tarantella saw that he was too far along to stop this time, she shifted and began rubbing herself off, gasping, "Me, too. Again," rubbing harder, he looking over Stella's shoulder at her, seeing her face contort with the pleasure of five separate lovers in her pussy, five lovers that were herself and more than herself. "I'm coming," he shouted, and Stella wrapped her legs about his ass, pulling him harder into the moistness of her.

For a few moments, then, he knew again who he really was.

Then, returning to the earth-level trip, he beamed at both girls and kissed each of them tenderly on the pussy lips. "You angels," he said sincerely.

"Christ, I love to masturbate," Tarantella said happily. "Christ, it's as good as fucking sometimes."

She leaned over and kissed Stella. Then each of them kissed the doctor's penis one more time.

"I love you both," he said.

"And I love both of you," Stella said, "Far out!"

Ten minutes later, fully dressed, clean-shaven, bright-eyed and in his right mind, Dr. Roger Prong stepped on the gas and zoomed away to another day at Orgasm Research, secure that his scientific objectivity could stand any strain placed upon it.

The sky was blue and he smiled at it. The world was a good place to be.

THE END

Tracking Down the Mama Vibe: Sexual Fantasy and the Nature of Magical Fiction

Afterword by Gregory Arnott

For the Father and the Son
The Holy Spirit is the norm;
Male-female, quintessential, one,
  Man-being veiled in woman-form.
Glory and worship in the highest,
  Thou Dove, that deifiest,
Being that race, most royally run
To spring sunshine through winter storm.
Glory and worship be to Thee,
Sap of the world-ash, wonder-tree!

  -from Liber XV: Ecclesiæ Gnosticæ Catholicæ Canon
            Missæ, "The Gnostic Mass"

"There are those who will find this manual to be insufficiently titillating or pornographic . . . there will be others who are astute enough to treasure this . . . as a rare rariora of authentic Sex Magick . . . they need no seven year itch of the intellect to stimulate the mind, to discover why and how Sex Magick works. It is the result of sincere and regular practice that counts." - Louis T. Culling, *Sex Magick*

Writing about magic, pornography or Robert Anton Wilson is a difficult proposition. The permanency of ink doesn't fit any of our trio of topics snugly. Writing about Robert Anton Wilson as a magician/pornographer compounds the difficulty. In my mind, we need to begin by discussing the idea of Wilson as a magician or occultist, the intricacies of which goes beyond the purview of this afterword; suffice it to say that Wilson was heavily involved in formal magical practices at the time of the publication of *The Sex Magicians.* Happily enough, after having read Wilson's first foray into published fiction, I don't need to convince the reader of his credentials as a pornographer. This slim volume contains some top notch smut, yeah? Enough to get you thinking, at least; but I think Wilson, like the Divine Marquis, merely baited the hook with his randy proto-*Illuminatus!* protagonists. The sex is to draw all three of your eyes towards the Church of Scientific Illumination; it's in the title, after all. Come for the taboo physicality, stay for the taboo magick.

Sex magic(k) is the most titillating tautology in all of magic. We have a whole secret society based around the idea of hiding the exact secret to fucking and succeeding. Everyone can do it, but there seems to be something missing in most of our loin sneezes. The magical wank has become a popular enough idea in magic that many think it is the basic premise of magical practice: one amusingly ingenious interpretation of *The Sex Magicians* even posited that the novel was published to crank Illuminatus! into public existence. Exuding private energy into the public sphere is a charming idea; the premise of sex magic is so simple, yet so hard, to talk about. Perhaps that is the best place to begin an explanation of where sex and magic intersect at their most obvious levels in the circa-1973 life of Robert Anton Wilson.

Wilson's "general magical period" would have extended from the time he read Regardie's *The Eye in the Triangle* to somewhere in the early eighties. During this period, his *specific* term of practice would have accompanied the years after being introduced to Crowley, his involvement with the New Reformed Order of the Golden Dawn, throughout the Sirius communications/hallucinations while rubbing shoulders with various shadowy luminaries up until the year preceding the tragic, profound events recounted at the end of *Cosmic Trigger.* As Blake or any other magician worth their salt will tell you, profundity often begins in silliness. And the occult milieu at the end of the Sixties was a true peacock's tail, in the alchemical sense. The ultraviolet brilliance of expression became saturated and heavy with the consequences of thwarted desire. Experience dyed the shining hues of possibility and idealism to something that resembled darkness and ridiculousness. At the time *The Sex Magicians* was published it was unsurprising that something containing kernels of the magnificent truth of the imagination, namely magic, would have been wrapped in the gauzy, quite Felicien-Ropsy veil of pornography.

Wilson isn't exactly known for the subtlety of his sex scenes in the first place, and what is contained in *The Sex Magicians* is little more than the "perversities" contained in *Schrodinger's Cat, Masks of the Illuminati* or the original *Illuminatus!*. Rocket-like cocks and hot snatches abound. But the provenance of *The Sex Magicians* can't be limited to the do-whatever-you-please permissiveness of the counterculture or the boys' club atmosphere of the Playboy offices; magic was quite smutty at the time all on its own, thank you very much. The vast majority of occult-eroticism was the drab type of stuff one could easily produce from an AI art generator or a fanart message board today. Maybe a little more intentional in its creation and distribution, but ultimately uninspiring. Yet there were truths hidden deep in the trash. Pearls in Pornocrates' wallow. Wilson himself relates that *Sex, Drugs and the Occult*, published the same year as *The Sex Magicians*, was initially shortened to *Sex & Drugs: A Journey Beyond Limits* as Hugh Hefner believed that, and I'm paraphrasing, only homosexuals and women bought books on the occult. Some of the intrinsic value of the literature of that time is its sheer shamelessness and sensationalism, such as *The Memoirs of Aleister Crowley* by James Harvey (1967), which

is described by Professor Tracy Tupman as little more than
an excuse to insert digressive fictional sexual encounters in
between feeble bits of truths about Crowley's life. On the
other hand, sometimes we can find some stars in the gutters
and find some glimpses of a more liberated sense of truth and
worth, where the mundane contains the supernal. Malkuth is
in Kether and Kether in Malkuth, in another manner. Francis
King, Wilson's favorite "non-paranoid" occult author, writes
about a novel, *Inpenetrable* (sic), described as "a novel dealing
with, of all things, the Hermetic Order of the Golden Dawn"
in which "[t]he author . . . has shifted the Golden Dawn
date to 1969 and situated its headquarters in Eaton Square."
So, it isn't surprising to find a missive for the Church of
Scientific Illuminism in a book driven by metaphysical-erotic
forces generated by a sexpot attached to an extraordinarily
well-endowed Sybian in an office along early-seventies Lake
Shore Drive; really, it's all par for the course.

Where did Wilson's practice of sex magic originate?
Not from *The Eye in the Triangle* or Crowley's writings,
the former of which is not practice-oriented and the latter
of which was scant and opaque at the time, nor from the
aforementioned magical wank/sigilization technique. As far
as I know, Wilson doesn't mention Osman Spare, the much
(self-) abused whipping boy of chaos magick, who really does
deserve much better. Wilson tells his readers in the margins
of *Cosmic Trigger* and *Sex, Drugs & Magick* that the formula
of sex magick is obvious if one but reads between the lines of
Crowley's texts. For those of us too nearsighted to see between
said lines, he recommends the text *Sex Magick* by Louis T.
Culling. Wilson never struck me as a reader or practitioner who
stuck to formalism or descriptivism; that seems against his holy
schtick. So it isn't exactly fair to say that because he references
a book a couple of times it was where he derived his practice.
But I do believe that he thought it was worth consideration,
and that there was practical value therein for the reader: Wilson
was nothing if not considerate and earnest. And he was always

one ready to point out the humor of things, and with Louis T. Culling, that's not too terribly difficult.

Louis T. Culling was a student/devotee of C.F. Russell, one of Crowley's many erstwhile student/devotees.* Russell was an American mathematician and enthusiastic enough convert to remove himself to the Abbey of Thelema in Sicily during its brief span before Loveday's death and Mussolini's dictatorship. He left before the moldering end, though, supposedly repulsed by Aleister's "Alice" persona. Back in America he founded, or was the spiritual center of, the Choronzon Club which transformed into (or from!) the Great Brotherhood of God. What can I say? The man had a gift for idiotic names. Eventually, Russell, knight exemplar of insane *I Ching* calculations and suspected supreme sorcerer of salaciousness, might have met Louis T. Culling. I say "might have" because Culling is a liar. All magicians are liars, but that is beside the point right now: the point is that Culling isn't a very convincing liar. Yet, Wilson recommends him.

~•~

* Reportedly, he was also an acquaintance of Charles Stanfield Jones, better known as Frater Achad, Crowley's lost magical son.

~•~

Regardie revealed the secret rituals of the Golden Dawn because he feared they would be lost unto history, a similar reason to Aleister Crowley's publication of their secret rituals in *The Equinox*. They both also wanted cash. Presumably, Culling's motivation behind publishing the secrets of the G. B G. was similarly holistically altruistic and individualistically satisfying. Culling, in *Sex Magick,* writes about a technical, three-degree system of initiation into the full realization of the truest expression of "divided for the sake of union." And I'm pretty sure it was so he could share a multilayered masturbation fantasy about the success of the magical process.

Culling is the only author I know who is as wrapped up

in the batshit authenticity of his own bullshit as Kenneth
Grant, the late claimant to the throne of the O.T.O., as well as
sharing Grant's qualities of being extremely entertaining and
illuminating. In *Sex Magick* and *The Complete Curriculum of
the Great Brotherhood of God*, Culling sets out a system of
mystical enlightenment through a curriculum of Thelemic sex
magic. The skeleton of the system is taken from Crowley's
initiatory teaching concerning sex magick and is similar
enough to non-sanctioned publications of the secret O.T.O.
rituals that there has to be some element of verisimilitude to the
real thing. There is also a good reason to believe that most of
the trappings and theoretical explanations are embellishments
of Culling's, Russell's or parties unknown. Grady McMurtry,
the official pick for leadership of Crowley's Ordo Templi
Orientis, was so incensed by Culling's spilling of the beans
and bud-wills that he said: "I would not care to have the karma
of a Lou Culling who published certain (inaccurate) books on
sex Magick. That is like handing a lighted stick of dynamite
to a child for a fire cracker, or throwing acid tabs to teenagers
like sugar cubes to piss-ants. The only thing I can think of
worse from a Thelemic point of view is telepathic hypnosis.
You will notice that Crowley was never so irresponsible." Let's
hope it didn't come to that for Louis Culling. who wrote in the
"Apologia" for *Sex Magick* that he took "full responsibility,
magickally" for the consequences of the supposed secrets of
the G.B.G. McMurtry also didn't have a very high opinion of
another cat-escaping-bag volume that was surely influential
on Wilson's understanding of sex magick: Francis King's *The
Secret Rituals of the O.T.O.*. Secret organizations never like
books that leak their "secrets": indirectly, accurately, obscured
or marred. Wilson, to a degree, respected and somewhat
believed in the exercises and history laid out by arch-weirdos
such as Culling and Grant. This gives us a glimpse into the
wild, hairy, moist and willing magic of *The Sex Magicians*.

Another bit of Culling's oeuvre that gives us insight into the
prestidigitation of Wilson's first novel is the magical letter to

the Penthouse that appears in *Sex Magick*. It is a farce of the highest order and I am much obliged to Mr. Culling and all spirits invoked, evoked and involved in the process that led this vignette into print. Truly, Culling pens an absurd, all-American tall tale concerning an initiate of his order who improbably changed his name to "Lou" for the sake of anonymity. And with a focus reminiscent of Kierkegaard, our author gives us a tale of *bud-wills***, a pair of sexual dynamo sisters down on their luck and splay-legged in their gratitude, illegal wolf-breeding and the proof that Louis' magick system really works.

~•~

** To give an inadequate explanation: a "bud-will" is a figure of speech that depicts a "child," the metaphorical result of sexual alchemy. It is the intelligence that carries out the ethereal machinations that will be about the will of the magician. Culling is fond of the term, which Crowley mostly uses in *Liber Aleph*. Wilson refers to *Liber Aleph* occasionally, but most explicitly in naming the chapter of *Masks of the Illuminati* after the titles of the sermon-lectures in that book. (Interestingly enough, those sermon-lectures are addressed to Stanfield Jones from Crowley.)

~•~

Wilson drank at this well and surely, with his nose to the grindstone of *Playboy* submissions within the same span of time, could catch the musk of sexual fantasy run amok. Yet our author recommends *Sex Magick*, so I'd recommend looking into this volume if you wish to understand the possible profundity of *The Sex Magicians*. Here, I should also say that I would recommend reading the early volumes of Kenneth Grant's so-called "Typhonian Trilogies"; the original Trilogy, Episodes IV-VI, if you will. Grant was mad, delightful and keen to another world that he both convincingly and ridiculously details in his oeuvre. And unsurprisingly, he writes with varying degrees of convincingness about various scandalous sexual practices. To discuss his life and work would require a separate work, but suffice it to say herein that Wilson also drank from that bucket as a burgeoning magician.

I am tempted, like McMurtry, to say that sex and magic are not toys. Yet, that's exactly how they should be regarded in the best sense; the best and brightest of tools to explore the possibilities and boundaries of our shared worlds. Sex and magic, as well as drugs for that matter, remind me of fireworks; supremely entertaining and terribly fun until something goes wrong. All of these things invite reckless sensibilities and yearning for bigger returns. They are certainly dangerous if they are played with imprudently or with reckless abandon, yet a sense of abandon is needed to truly appreciate their possibilities. It is a delicate balance, but within the imagination we need not fear the missing bits of body, mind or soul that come from life's extravagances. We can experiment to our heart's content and need not worry about the marriage of Joe Smith, American, nor the propriety of Mary Kelly's family: we need not fear the Mama Vibe. Instead, these imaginary scenarios let us reflect upon the world inside ourselves and how it interconnects with the exterior world. With our magic, we are able to change the course of our lives based on the knowledge of many lives and possibilities that we have lived already in the confines of a less permanent world. We can regrow the toes, fingers and more precious appendages we blow off in our dreams. We can, through our imaginations, become more impeccable in the so-called "real" world. In the pseudo-pornographic *Fireworks*, the late, great, flaming Kenneth Anger had his protagonist arise with blazing scrawls before his eyes, hinting at the waking illumination our nocturnal emissions might allow. The mobile lens of imagination in the mobile element of the wake world; we are free to play, all the wiser after the experience of our infinite lives; and then, Oh! – the possibilities!

And in the realm of our "real" worlds, we need to exercise intelligently and abandon ourselves where we may, in alignment with our true will. I would be majorly remiss to write about Wilson's understanding and practice of sex magic without bringing up the presence of his partner, Arlen Riley Wilson. Given the queenly title of "the Most Beautiful Woman in the Galaxy" by Wilson in *Cosmic Trigger*, our author painstakingly points out that his truest magical experiences came about with her willing assistance. After speaking with Prop Anon, the musician and Wilson biographer, he confirmed my notion that Wilson was faithful to Arlen throughout their marriage. (Or, no evidence or anecdotes exist that suggest otherwise.) I bring this up not to shame anyone whose relationship model is different than Wilson's, but rather to point out that the boundaries between fantasy and reality can be kept firm. Your level of abandon/indulgence/experimentation is up to your own sensibilities and boundaries as well as the ever present need for the consideration of the feelings and safety of other people. But in our fantasies, we can explore desire, "perversion," and ourselves in ways that are less comfortable in the world of others and consequences. In both worlds, remember: Do what thou wilt shall be the whole of the Law.

It is startlingly, if not surprisingly, easy to become lost in the wake world, let alone the world of imagination which we coequally, if somewhat more ignorantly, inhabit. It is a good thing that we have a trick to find our bearings in the hinterlands of the mind, which is simply adopting a framework of where we might be. Some models are more useful than others; one that Robert Anton Wilson found useful during times in his life was the Qabalistic (. . . Cabalistic, Kabbalistic etc.) Tree of Life. The Tree of Life is a cartographic glyph of fantasy cosmology and upon its sephira and paths, its veils and absences, a traveler can measure their distance in the interior and exterior universes. Your mileage may vary, but if we are to entertain some basic Qabalistic orienteering it is quite a simple task to locate *The Sex Magicians;* not only as a product of the cultural space and time in which it was published, but also as the novel's metaphysical provenance and place of its action.

The Sex Magicians hails from and takes place within Yesod, the sphere of the moon.

Yesod, according to luminaries such as Will Parfitt and Alan Moore, is explicitly said to be the realm of the imagination, the lower unconscious and *sexual fantasy*. It is perhaps in the late Steve Moore's exquisite *Somnium* that we have a perfect expression of the delicate lunar dance of sex and imagination. Fantasy, in its truest sense. Both magic and sexuality are explicitly about desire and the expression thereof; perhaps that is why they are both seen as something to be avoided when we are in polite society. *Somnium* is an incredibly sexual novel in which nothing *explicitly* sexual happens and yet is loaded with the pure intent of magical power, a literary equivalent of *coitus reservatus*; *The Sex Magicians* is the literary equivalent of occult bukkake. But the substance of both shines with the same pearlescent, lunar sheen. So, if you'd like to expand your exploration of potent magical smut, head towards Steve Moore. You won't laugh as much at *two* perfect blowjob scenes (Hef's farcical charicature's name is "Sput!"), but you might end up weeping over the end of a dream. Both pieces of fiction are examples of the opening of the thirty-second path, through one of its "easiest" avenues.

In the lush publication *25,000 Years of Erotic Freedom*, originally, and superiorly, a spiritedly spiteful essay titled "Bog Venus vs. Nazi Cock Ring," magician-pornographer Alan Moore relates that William Blake was himself a magician-pornographer. Like-finds-like. To the world's sorrow, Blake's pornography was burnt at the behest of his young disciples, concerned for their weird, old mentor's legacy, by Blake's partner Catherine. When Blake penned his unearthly, holy writ poetry the world was a vile, boring and mundane place. Blake painted and wrote his porn amidst this in the pursuit of a more free and pure art. A more pure and full world. His art is undeniably magical. In the contrast of survey and hindsight, Robert Anton Wilson wrote something pornographic and puerile and wove in threads of wisdom.

When Wilson mentions a specific song, a reader is well-advised
to *listen*. Notice that Buffy Saint Marie weaves through this
fiction, reminding us that behind all the festivities and facades,
there is God and Magic. And in another manner, God and
Magic are the Festivities and the Facades. This is the bottom
line, y'all. Guerilla tactics. When Wilson wrote this book, it
wasn't meant for posterity; it went below the radar and wasn't
seemingly necessary. In our psychedelic swirled world of
instant pornography and spiritual depredation, this might be
a godsend. By Chance or Providence, we have it now and it's
time to heed the call of its revolution. It's time to start thinking
with our dicks.*** To think with our two heads, our third eyes
charged with energized enthusiasm for whatever the Mother
Goddess or Nature's God demand of ourselves, and, our self.

~•~

*** This is and isn't meant to be glib. We have to remember
that in *Book 4*, that work that was editorially feted by Wilson
in *Masks of the Illuminati*, Crowley dubs the ritual wand the
"baculum" throughout the volume. As a young man who
strived to forge his own "baculum," I was chagrined to learn
it was the Latin term for the bone present in many mammals'
penises. Also, a big "Thank You, Ma'am" to Michelle Olley
for taking care of the social-temporal context for the book
because I was not up to that task. Do what thou wilt shall be
the whole of the Law . . . and all that shit.

~•~

About Gregory Arnott

Gregory Arnott is a magician, writer, teacher and a
major figure in his own mind. Even within the lurid
non-boundaries of his private world, he knows he stands
on the shoulders of much better humans. Currently, he is at
large with a beloved wife, daughter and two cats. Having
read Wilson from far too young of an age, he'd like to think
he's learned a thing or two. And yet, he suspects he hasn't.

HILARITAS
PRESS

Publishing the Books of Robert Anton Wilson
and Other Adventurous Thinkers
www.hilaritaspress.com